TEMPT

A SECRETS AND LIES NOVEL

AINSLEY BOOTH

ABOUT THIS BOOK

The hot guy in a suit across the aisle isn't Hazel's type. He's the cold-day-in-hell type she knows all about. But when their train gets stuck on the tracks and day turns into a long, cold night, Sam's devilish smile is hard to resist.

The woman sitting across from him isn't interested in small talk. Or any kind of talking, and Sam is fine with that. So what if he can't stop looking at her? Wondering about her? She's not interested. End of story. Until a snowstorm traps them in the middle of nowhere, and the night stretches ahead of them.

She doesn't want to talk. Maybe they could find a game to pass the time. Something secret and special and limited to one night only—but a decade-old secret may spoil the fun.

Tempt is a standalone romance about Sam and Hazel. It is also the first book in a two-book duet that concludes with a separate novel about Grace and Luke.

HAZEL

WHAT DOES a thirty-one-year-old self-sufficient woman do when her parents "break the news" that they won't be home for Christmas because they're going on a cruise to the Caribbean?

Click her heels and happily book an extravagant trip for one to an over-the-top luxury lodge in the middle of a real-life snow globe, that's what.

And I cannot wait.

I just need to get there, which is easier said than done. I didn't like the idea of renting a car and driving eight hours by myself, so I decided to take the train—and when one lives in a small town, that means catching a connecting train in the city.

And dealing with city people.

No offense to city people, but there's a reason I moved to a small town—one with a walkable downtown and frequent train service to the city, of course.

I arrived in Toronto this morning on the first train from

Stratford. Then I had a couple of meetings, a lovely tea for one at the King Eddie, and now I'm back at Union Station to catch another train. This one will head to Ottawa.

I adore the train. I can work, drink, and daydream, and someone else worries about getting me safely to my destination. The only thing I need to do is get myself to the gate on time, which is enough of a challenge.

Toronto's downtown train hub is packed full of sweaty people and oversized suitcases, with wet spots all over the floor from melting snow. All of that makes navigation through the crowd extra-precarious. It's three days before Christmas and there's a storm brewing, so everyone who needs to get out of the city for the holidays is trying to do it now.

I dodge around a group of university students in the middle of the concourse and join the line of passengers queued up at the gate.

I'm the last to board the business class car at the front of the train. After carefully stowing my carry-on, I make my way down the car, looking for my seat. I should have a seat to myself. I always do.

Every trip, apparently, except this one. I silently groan as I realize I'm in a backwards-facing seat—fine—across from someone else.

Less fine. I don't want to share my table.

I see a dark head of hair. Masculine hair, as much as one can anticipate that sort of thing. The long leg and big arm overflowing the generous seat is a warning sign, too. Some slick businessman, it looks like, taking up far too much space in what was going to be my writing cocoon for the next four hours.

Well, I hope he likes silence, because I'm going to ignore the fuck out of him.

He doesn't look up as I move past and dump my messenger bag on my seat. Coat off, computer out.

And it's because I have that emotional armour up—I'm focused on ignoring my seatmate and getting my work done —that when I sit down, and his dark gaze locks on my face with a blazing intensity, I don't react.

We're strangers. I owe him nothing. In the spirit of the season, I flash a polite but dismissing smile and take my seat.

Headphones up and on. Plug in the cord. Open the computer.

I ignore the weird hiccup in my pulse. Ignore the man, and his searing gaze, which he's now thankfully dropped.

(Okay, I only know this because I looked up again. For a split-second. Curiosity will kill me as surely as it killed the cat.)

I'm not sure what I'm feeling right now. Deja vu, but not really. A weird disconnect because I'd filled in a generic proto-man as my seatmate when I saw the suit, the arm and leg taking up too much space, the roughly slicked-back, sharply side-parted haircut.

You noticed a lot about his hair. More than I'd realized, and something in my belly quivers.

His haircut doesn't matter.

His face, his gaze, that unsettling sizzle—none of it matters.

I open my files and give myself a goal. Three more revisions before the porter comes around with the first round of drinks. Then I can close this project and free-scrawl anything I want for my blog. Write drunk, edit sober—advice not meant to be taken literally, but it's never steered me wrong.

But the words on the screen swim in front of my eyes.

It takes a painfully long stretch of time to get into my task. Two glasses of red wine help with my concentration. Help to slow down my racing pulse and finally, thankfully, crystallize my attention.

An hour later my revisions are done. It's not the best work I've ever done, but it's entertaining and hot. Good enough. I fire the document off to my editor with a note that I'll be out of the office for the next four days and would be happy not to get it back for the final pass until after the new year.

Then I sneak a quick glance across the table. At *him*. He's still buried in his phone. His hair is ridiculous. He probably spends more on his cuts than I do mine.

His suit looks expensive. So do his shoes, his tie... I'd rather imagine him in jeans. Fitted ones that hug his thighs. A Henley with the sleeves rolled up, revealing his forearms. Corded, tan from time in the sun. A light dusting of dark hair that looks soft and feels softer.

I can't help it.

This is what I do. I see people and they turn into sex in my head. It was only in the last few years that I figured out I could actually do something with the super dirty vignettes that form unbidden in my mind.

Jeans, a rolled up shirt sleeve. That burning gaze—there's a lot to work with there.

No words, no explanations. Just a hot sex scene set to a dirty, thuddy beat.

We're in a dance club, yelling over the music, and then, when that proves frustrating, Mr. Searing Gaze takes me—no, not me—takes my character by the hand—no, the wrist, his fingers hot and firm as they manacle around her flesh—and leads her to a nook off a dark hallway.

I write and re-write, typing words quickly, then deleting some of them before madly dashing out more.

The dark hallway is still loud. Too loud to be heard, but that's not his goal. He wanted privacy, and now they have some.

He asks with his body—can he touch her? Should he kiss her?

Yes. No. Do it anyway. She leans in anyway and gives him her mouth, her legs, a grind of her sex. He finds her waist, then higher. Her breasts. Her nipples, and then—

The train slows to a halt. I lift my hands off the keyboard, the fantasy word blitz temporarily pausing.

I glance out the window, but there's nothing to be seen. No lights, no town. No stop was announced, and we're only an hour and a half outside of Toronto. Not quite to Kingston. Maybe we need to let another train pass before we can continue.

The perfect head of hair doesn't look up.

I take a deep breath and go back to the story, but without the white noise of the train rushing along the tracks, I can't do it. As if he could hear the filthy words I'm spinning on this side of my computer screen if it were too quiet in our little mini compartment.

Maybe I don't need to write anything else tonight anyway. I've got enough for a Christmas gimme to my blog followers. I'll polish this up when I get to the hotel, then post it before bed.

Then the train jerks backwards, and my computer skitters off the table between us, sliding precariously towards the aisle.

He catches it deftly, and I stand up, reaching for it. "Sorry." My heart pounds in my chest, because *oh God he's holding porn about himself*, but he doesn't know that.

"It's not your fault," he says, handing it over.

And then the train jerks again, forwards this time, and I tumble back into the leather seat, clutching my laptop to my chest.

He swears under his breath and looks around, then back to me. "Are you all right?"

"I'm fine." I peer out the window again, but it's pitch-black out there and bright in here. I can't see anything. "That was… sudden. Twice."

"Yeah." He looks me over, like he's sizing me up. Both for injuries—and I really am fine—and also for how to handle this new talking thing. I smile tightly and take off my headphones, which had fallen around my neck in the whole yanking forwards and back anyway. He taps on his phone screen, then rolls his neck with a groan. "There's been a collision up ahead on the tracks."

"How do you know?"

He turns the phone screen so I can see it. Twitter. "Hashtags."

I'm not sure why the train staff haven't said anything. "Maybe it's just a short interruption to service."

"Maybe."

I clutch my computer tighter.

"Are you sure you're okay?"

"Yep."

"Good. I—" He's interrupted by the intercom.

"Bon soir..." The announcement was read out in French first, which I don't speak, so I listened patiently until it repeated in English. *"Good evening, ladies and gentleman. We apologize for the sudden stop. We have a delay on the tracks ahead and have received instructions to hold position here for the moment."*

Damn it. He was right. "That's too bad," I say quietly, my heart sinking. Of course I hope whoever is in the collision is all right, and this could just be a short delay until they get the tracks cleared.

"I guess, uh…" He gives me a rueful smile, like he knows that I didn't want to talk, but now we're talking anyway, so the polite thing to do is do it right. "Can I introduce myself?"

My sinking heart jolts back into place. It's an odd request, but I like it. I smile. "Sure."

"I'm Sam. Sam Preston."

I nod. Okay. Let's do this. I hold out my hand. "I'm Aibhlin."

THAT'S ALL HE GETS. My writing nom de plume, and only the first name at that. I don't give him my last name. I don't want him to google me with the same speed he found the news about the train stoppage.

"A pleasure, Aibhlin." He repeats it exactly right, his pronunciation perfect. *Aveline.* No weird reaction, no questions. His gaze doesn't leave my face, and his smile seems sincere.

I relax a bit. "Same to you, Sam."

Then I put my computer in my bag, because who am I kidding? I'll be too on edge to write any more words tonight.

And if we're going to do this, I'm going to do it right.

He gives me another smile. This one is bolder. Inviting, seductive. *Do you want to play a game? Flirt instead of work?*

I don't. Not really. I didn't, anyway.

I glance at his hand. No ring. Means nothing, but I'm jaded now. I always check. "Heading to Ottawa for work?"

He nods.

I pick up the stemless wine glass that holds the remnants of my second drink. "And what do you do, Sam Preston?"

The corner of his mouth pulls up, forming an almost-dimple right at the point. Does he like the full name treatment? "I'm an investment banker."

I can't help it. I laugh. "Of course."

He gestures down at his suit. "Predictable?"

"Entirely."

"And you?"

Before I can answer—and who am I kidding, I wasn't

going to anyway—the door between the train cars clatters open behind me.

I turn and look at the steward, who is pushing the drinks cart. Just in the nick of time.

"Sorry about that, folks. I was in the next car over and it took some time to get back. You heard the announcement? We're going to be here for a bit."

"What's the problem?" Sam asks, as if he doesn't already know from Twitter.

The attendant doesn't give us a real answer. "A delay on the tracks is all I've been told so far." He gestures to the cart. "Good thing we're well stocked. Can I get you another drink, miss? And then I'll be back with dinner service shortly."

Miss. My lips twitch and I hold out my glass. "Top me up. And keep calling me miss, I like that."

"Of course." He gives me a generous pour, then turns to Sam, who so far into this trip has declined service. "And you, sir?"

Sam exhales roughly. "Well, if we're going to be here for a while, I'll take a rye on the rocks. Make it a double."

That's more like what I expected. Investment banker. Make it a double. There's something reassuring there. I know what to do with a man like this. Play with him, have my fun. Under no circumstances will I trust him, but that's all right.

Trust is overrated.

Once we're alone again, Sam lifts his glass in a toast. "To comfort while we wait."

I drink to that. "I hope nobody is hurt too badly."

"Same." He takes a big swallow, his throat working quickly

to down the fiery alcohol. No hesitation. Then he gestures to the window, where it's started snowing. Big, fat, swirling flakes of white brush against the window. "Maybe the tweets are wrong. Maybe the train is stopped for another reason, like the weather."

I'd like that. No injuries, no accident that's ruined a family's night.

"A storm," I murmur, my imagination twisting the newly swirling snow into a monster. "Ice demons."

I love the look of surprise on Sam's face as his brows hit the roof. "Ice demons?"

"I like it better than an accident three days before Christmas."

He shrugs. "Fair enough. There you go. So they've whipped up a weather system right in front of us? Iced the tracks and now we can't move forward?"

"Something like that." I hadn't meant to say ice demons out loud.

But Sam is rolling with it. "Are they angry at the train for some reason, or are we caught in between a battle between foes?"

And because he's into the story, so am I. "They could be fighting over a woman on the train? Or maybe it's one ice demon, and his beloved is on here somewhere. She's the only one who knows why we've stopped. And she's..." I lick my lips, trying to get it just right. What would she be feeling?

"Torn?"

"Terrified," I correct him. "This is the end of their story, maybe, and it feels like a life-or-death flight on her part. Now he's stopped her, trapped all these people."

"She's scared of him?"

I shake my head. "No. But she's scared of what he makes her feel."

He smiles. "You're a romantic."

"Only on the page."

"Ah. Touché."

Sorry to disappoint, buddy. I live in the real world. "How about you?"

He rolls his shoulders back, flexing inside his three-thousand-dollar suit jacket. No, he doesn't like romance. The jacket, the wolfish smile, the practiced way of offering to buy a woman a drink just to pass the time by—this guy is just as jaded about people as I am. He knows what's what. "I like the idea of it," he finally says. "In theory. But I think there's a solid chance the big scary demon is, in fact, the bad guy. I guess I hope that it all works out in an unexpected way in the end. Maybe the romance is—" He cuts himself off.

I'm not sure what we're talking about anymore. What happened to dirty flirting?

He immediately looks sideways, releasing me. He's good. Knows just how far to push, then pulls back. He wants to keep this fun, and frankly, I'm grateful for that. We could be here for hours.

His gaze locks on something—nothing, but he's pretending—out in the darkness. Beyond the sleeting white stuff, past the tree line.

To our imaginary boogeyman. To the territorial hero,

stalking the train out of misguided but romantic affection for a heroine.

"What happens next?" he asks, his voice low enough that this is just for us. The other passengers can't hear it. "On the page. With this ice demon and his beloved, stuck on the train."

"She knows the ice demon is upset. And she's worried that he doesn't know the strength of his own abilities." I like the way Sam leans in as I start weaving the story. I don't want to like it too much, but there's something about the look in his eye that emboldens me. Like he'll like anything I say here, I can be as wild as I want with this fantasy tale. "Maybe he doesn't know that a storm can interfere with travel plans, cause car accidents, or down power lines."

And that's when the lights in our car flicker and go out.

I DON'T GASP. Other people do, further down the train car, and then I hear Sam chuckle.

"That was a neat trick," he says as he taps his phone, lighting up the space between us weakly. I refocus my eyes on his grin. "What next, storyteller?"

"The ice demon takes a nap and the lights came back on," I say under my breath, but no such luck. I take a sip of wine. "Our heroine realizes she needs to find a way to communicate with the ice demon."

"Whoa, hold up, we've got a major plot hole." Sam clears his throat. "With all due respect to the narrator. But how did they fall in love if they can't talk?"

"Well he's not always in the form of a giant ice demon conjuring a storm. When he's not upset, he's like…seven feet tall and built like a cross between an NFL and an NBA player. And whatever he touches turns a little bit cold. Like he makes you shiver with each stroke, every caress."

"Sexy," Sam deadpans. He lifts his glass and takes another big swallow of rye, then wipes his mouth. My eyes have adjusted to the dim light, the entire car dark except for electronic glows here and there. It's eerie and intimate at the same time.

But more importantly, Sam doesn't understand the appeal of a sexy ice demon. I re-focus my attention. "You haven't had enough fun with—"

He reaches across the table and touches my hand. Hidden under his fingers is an ice cube, and the cold press against my skin makes me shiver exactly as I just explained.

"Ice," I whisper, finishing my thought.

"Tell me more about him," Sam murmurs, his eyes carefully watching me. "He's a man?"

"Some of the time." I suck in a breath as he moves his touch up my hand and onto my wrist.

"More?" His fingers slide onto the inside of my arm and I turn my hand over.

Yes, more.

He continues asking questions like he's not molesting my skin with a melting ice cube. "And the rest of the time?"

"Uh, he's a storm. Well, a larger-than-life man-shaped demon surrounded by a storm. He needs to take that shape regularly, although he can be an only slightly larger-than-life man most of the time."

"What happens in the summer?"

"You and your plot holes." I swallow hard. "He's gone in the summer. He has to travel somewhere cold."

"Brutal."

The lights flicker, and in a flash, Sam's touch is gone. By the time the train car is fully lit again, he's leaning back in his seat, the quintessential picture of the unconcerned man. I blink, adjusting to the brightness, and it's almost like all of that didn't just happen.

"*Bon soir...*" The announcement apologies for the temporary power interruption in French first, and then English. "*A power cable unhooked between the cars. The problem has been repaired, and your dinner service will begin shortly.*"

"No ice demon," I say.

Sam almost smirks, but he reins it in at the last second. "Are you disappointed?"

I don't answer him. Instead, I drain my wine glass.

"Do you want another drink?" He twists around, looking for the attendant.

I take a deep breath. "Probably shouldn't."

He smiles again, a slow and dangerous grin. "Probably not."

A hot, needy tug pulls low in my belly.

His gaze slides down my body as if he knows what the wolfish smile does to me inside. Then he snaps his eyes back to my face. "Do you want to play it safe, *Aibhlin?*"

The inflection is more effective than a bucket of ice water on my libido. My back straightens, and I tighten my legs.

No more languid fun. This train can get moving any time now. We didn't even get to dinner. "Oh, Sam. Why did you have to go and say it like that? Our game was so lovely there for a hot second."

His face tightens up. "Is that what it was to you? Some kind of game?"

"Of course. And it was for you, too. Obviously, with your *'I'm Sam. Sam Preston,'* nonsense."

His eyes flick to the window, to the now more chaotic snow and the darkness beyond. When he looks back, his smile is more familiar. Rueful.

Boyish, like I remember it from ten years ago.

2

SAM

Ten years earlier

"WHAT UP, PRESTON?"

I barely have the door open to my apartment when the guys shoulder their way in. Some of them, anyway. Not the whole crew.

I've been pissing people off lately, so when I put out the blast that I want to go out and get wasted tonight, I didn't know who would show.

Frankly, I don't give a fuck who's up for it or not.

Regan has a new boyfriend. Her prerogative. Good for her. All I need to do is get laid tonight and everything will be right with the world again.

Go and find Hazel in the library. No, not that.

Pursuing Regan's best friend is a bad idea. The worst.

The hottest, too.

Hazel with the knowing eyes and the wet little mouth. Hazel with the filthy jokes.

Which is why I need drinks tonight, and a lot of them. Because if I'm sober, I won't be able to shut down my brain, the obnoxious part of it that thinks and spins and calculates the odds until I can figure out how to bend them in my favour.

I can wear Hazel down. Of course I can. She's a dirty girl, deep down, and nobody else knows that about her. I'm the only one who knows her secret. I don't even fucking know how I know that, but I do. I see her. We're more alike that Hazel would like.

That's how I know.

She's me, only not fucked up. She's me, without the cards and booze and the money.

She's me, except she likes herself.

I grab the bottle of Jack off the counter. "This is what's up, motherfuckers. We are almost at the end of our collegiate careers, you jackoffs. We are going to celebrate tonight."

"Fuck yeah."

Fuck yeah. The motto to my entire university career. And if I get out of it alive, it'll be a fucking miracle. I pour a round of shots, welcoming the familiar burn.

One more term. Five more C+ papers, five more exams, and a passing attendance record, and I'll have the degree I need to access my trust fund. One more term, and I never need to speak to my parents again. Don't need to play their games.

Dark, bitter thoughts swirl through my head, and I chase them away with another shot of Jack.

WE HIT a club just south of campus, close enough it's more students than anyone else. I want to cut loose, I want to find some pussy. Those are my goals. But when I walk through the doors and I see a couple of guys who were a few years behind me at St. Mike's, guys I know have money to burn, I can't help the networker inside me.

"I'll catch up to you at the bar," I say to my friends, then swing wide to the second years clustered around a table. "Dylan, nice to see you, man." I take his hand, shaking it whether he wants to or not. Then I sling my arm around the neck of the guy next to him, whose name I cannot remember for the life of me, but I'm pretty sure I fucked his sister at her homecoming dance. She was not my date. It didn't matter. "Everyone having a good time tonight?"

I'm looking for a couple of things in a conversation like this. Recognition is key. If they don't know who I am and what kind of games I organize, I'm not going to tell them. My reputation is king. The rule is, I'm a nice guy. Approachable, friendly. But my games are hard to get into, and people need to ask.

Repeatedly.

None of these douchebags have asked yet, and I don't know if that's because my rep isn't as good with them as it should be, or if they're not sure they'll get into the game.

Dude-Whose-Sister-I-Banged, though, his eyes light up.

That's a great sign.

"Sam," he says, a little breathless. And his breath is whew, heavy with the vodka. Good, he won't remember that I don't know his name.

"What's up, bro?" I scruff him a little. "Haven't seen you around. You guys having a good time tonight?"

One of the others puffs his chest up. "Always."

"Great. Good." I wink and point finger guns at them all. "See you soon, buds."

An hour later, Dude-Whose-Sister-I-Banged shows up at the table we've scored. He's greedy, I can see it in his eyes. Behind him is a waitress with a bottle, and it's good stuff. He didn't cheap out.

"Guys," I say expansively. "Introduce yourselves to our new friend."

It works. They all shake his hand, and he tells each of them —unnecessarily—that his name is Cody. Cody Dewar. Over and over again, and then we drink his three-hundred dollar bottle of whiskey.

I'm barely into my second glass when I see Hazel at the bar.

She's looking at me, where I'm holding court, like I'm a piece of shit. She's not wrong.

I gesture for her to join us, and she shakes her head, but then something makes her change her mind, and she shrugs.

The way she stalks in our direction is fucking hot. Like she doesn't give a fuck if anyone thinks she's mad—she's not,

Hazel doesn't get mad. She just goes cold. The worst thing Hazel can give you is indifference. It fucking *cuts*.

And since she's bulldozing her way to my table, she is not indifferent. Not tonight. I'm grinning when she stops next to us.

"Cody," I bark. "There's a lady present. Get up and give her your seat."

She snorts. "I'm not staying. Just stopped by to remind Sam that he still has a paper due on Monday."

We had one class together in four years. It just ended. Well, it ends on Monday, but the joke's on Hazel. "I turned it in this afternoon."

Her eyes narrow. "You only started writing it yesterday."

"I know, I don't usually spend that much time on an assignment," I drawl. Then I stand up.

Cody tries to stand, too, but stumbles.

I shove him back into his seat.

He's misread the situation badly, because he thinks it's a good idea to tell Hazel she should smile more.

She acts like she didn't hear him. That indifference, whew. It hurts.

"I said—"

She leans right into his face and nods. "I heard your bro tip. I disregarded it immediately."

"A bro tip is a pro tip." He says it like it's fucking clever. It's not.

Hazel visibly cringes, and something hardens inside me. A need to prove to her I'm not that guy, even though I clearly am—or at least, I'm a guy happy to drink that guy's booze and take his money. "Can we talk?"

Her eyes flash. No. The answer is no. It has to be.

I move in and lower my voice. "Please." She watches my mouth. Maybe she didn't hear me over the music. I reach for her hand, circling my fingers around her wrist, and she doesn't pull away. "Come on," I say. Calculating the odds. Making my bet.

And when I tug, she follows.

We weave our way off the dance floor, through the sweaty, grinding crowd, and past the bar. Down the hallway.

My pulse is thumping now. Hard and fast. Heady.

She hops up onto a wooden ledge in a nook, where there used to be a payphone, and now it's a place for people to get up to no good in the shadows.

I want to get up to no good with Hazel. I want to bury my hand between her bare thighs and discover what her pussy feels like. If she has soft curls or bare skin, if she's already wet. Fuck, I don't know what would be hotter. If she'd already be ready for my fingers to slide deeper, or if she would need some coaxing.

There is zero chance she's going to let me finger fuck her in a club, but I want that so much it burns. I want her pussy juice to soak into my hand, so I can smell it as I get myself off later.

"You finished your paper already?"

"Sure did."

"Is it any good?"

"It's a pass." I drop my gaze to where her bare legs are bright in the relative darkness of our little nook.

"Sam." She says my name like she knows I'm a pervert, and she isn't impressed. "You wanted to talk?"

I wanted to get her alone so I could talk her into making a mistake with me. "It was too loud out there."

"Loud and gross. Those guys are obnoxious."

"Yeah." But they're the only people who can stand me anymore, so…fuck it. "They're my friends, though. Sorry."

She doesn't say anything to that.

She doesn't need to.

Fuck. "This isn't why I wanted to talk about."

"Did you want to talk, Sam?" The mockery drips off her voice. *Or did you want to fuck me in a dark hallway?*

Yes.

The answer is fucking yes.

"We keep bumping into each other."

"We go to the same school."

"I've seen you more in the last couple of weeks than usual."

"Maybe you're just noticing me for the first time."

Not at all. "We've been friends for a while."

She frowns.

I move closer. "Aren't we friends, Hazel?"

She licks her lips, a quick swipe of a pink tongue, and glances to the side. When she twists her head back, I'm closer still. There's little space between us now, and I drag in a rough breath, inhaling some of her scent.

"Maybe we're not exactly friends," I whisper.

And she fucking shudders. Hard, raw, real. With a gasp,

she scrambles back, but she's sitting on a ledge, her legs spread enough for me to wedge myself between them and brace my arms on either side of her.

"Don't run away," I growl.

She gives me a wide-eyed glare. "This isn't talking."

"I'm saying plenty." I smirk when she drops her gaze to my mouth. Oh, the things I want to do to her with my lips, my tongue, my teeth. "I want you. Can we talk about that?"

"Why?"

"Because you're pretty. Because you're smart. Because you tell the dirtiest jokes I've ever heard, and when everyone else is cackling, you go to a different place. You get a little dreamy." I brush my mouth against her cheek. "I want to be a part of your dirty dreams."

"I don't—" She cuts herself off, because *yes she does*.

I want to crow. "You're a dirty girl, aren't you?"

"Everyone is," she whispers. Then she turns her head and kisses me, her lips swollen and soft and perfect.

We kiss until she's breathless and I'm hard, my brain a little fuzzy, and I finally put my hands on her bare fucking thighs.

She trembles under my touch.

"You make me want to do filthy things, Hazel. You know that?"

She moans as my fingers stroke higher on her thighs. Almost there. I want her shaking by the time I touch her pussy.

I licked her neck. Fuck, she tastes good. "I wanted to do

this in the library. When you called me on my shit. Would you have let me then?"

She freezes.

"You wanted me in the library?" Her voice catches. "Weeks ago?"

There's a warning flag here, but I'm not following. "Fuck, yeah."

Wrong answer. Fuck me.

"No." She shoves me back, stronger than she looks. Shaking, she takes two steps back towards the pulsing dance floor. Then she stops and shoots me a *drop dead, asshole* look. "This can't happen, Sam. You're an asshole. And if you want a bro tip…those assholes aren't really your friends. But you know that, and you hang out with them anyway. So you know what? I'm done with you. If you *ever* see me again, pretend you don't know me."

3

SAM

Present Day

I DIDN'T SEE her again. She dodged me for an entire term and didn't show up at convocation.

What were the odds she would slide into the seat across from me a decade later?

She gave me a fake name, and that was fine. I did my part. I pretended not to know her, but I do—or did. Except she was into it, too.

Fuck.

And now she's staring at me like I've ruined everything. Again.

"None of your business," Hazel says, her eyes bright and challenging. "You started playing the game. I just took it to the next level. It's a shame for both of us you couldn't keep it there."

I genuinely thought I'd never see this woman again.

I was not prepared for this evening on any level.

And yet.

And *yet*, I can still feel it. The sizzle, the connection. The what-almost-was, the what-never-could-be. To be fair to the missed opportunity, none of that sizzle had existed for ninety-five percent of the time we knew each other.

She'd been Regan's best friend, and no matter how complicated and childish the relationship I'd had with my college girlfriend had been, I'd only had eyes for her.

And cards.

But no other women.

After it ended badly, so completely my fault, Hazel hated me for having hurt Regan. Fair enough.

So it had surprised the hell out of both of us when one day, there it was.

Sizzle.

Spark.

A connection neither of us saw coming. A mocking tone turned into a lighthearted tease in the library, and bam, I suddenly saw Hazel McLaughlin in a whole new light.

It took her longer to admit it. Three weeks longer, precisely.

"This can't happen, Sam. If you ever see me again, pretend you don't know me."

And she'd been right. It couldn't happen. Not then.

When she sat down across from me tonight, I did my best to respect that decade-old request. I let her work in silence, only looking at her when her head was down.

I *could* pretend I didn't know her. I couldn't stop myself

from looking at her. From stealing hungry, consuming glances when it was safe to, when she was lost in her work. I had to absorb the shock of her reappearance—temporary, fleeting, precarious—in minuscule slices.

Her hair is longer. Darker, too. More mid-range honey blonde, with lots of brown underneath. She has heavy bangs now, which suit her. Everything about her seems right, as much as I can say that about a woman who didn't want me anywhere in her life.

I shouldn't have traced the lines of her body as she curled up across from me. She'd worn a light, puffy parka over yoga pants and a hoodie for the train, and every inch was soft and touchable—by someone other than me, so that trick with the ice cube was offside.

Living up to the fantasy role of an untamed beast.

I'm a beast, all right.

And Hazel...

We couldn't be more different.

She seems, as she always did back in university, relentlessly real. She makes me feel like a fool for wearing business clothes on an evening train in the middle of a snowstorm.

She makes me feel like a fool because I'd forgotten how beautiful she is, exactly as she is—and now she's so much more so than back in the day.

I want to get to know this woman. I want to know why she dreams of ice demons, and what else makes her shiver.

I want to apologize for way back when, and convince her I'm worth knowing now, although I blew our game, so maybe I'm not.

That's as good a place as any to start. "You win," I say plainly. "I couldn't keep up. I forgot, for a second, that I'd made you that promise. But I'd remembered before that. I remembered when you sat down, and that was hard, because the second I realized it was you, after all these years, I wanted to say so much. I wanted to jump up and spill my guts out to you." I hold my arms wide. "And frankly, that is not something I'm entirely comfortable with. Even now. *What the fuck, Sam. She doesn't need to hear your story.* That's what I told myself. So I kept my mouth shut, and if we hadn't stopped, I'd have kept it shut. I remembered my promise, if that's worth anything."

Her eyes flit back and forth, assessing me. Then she shrugs. "It's a weird night."

That's it.

I dump all that on her, verbal spillage of the worst sort, and she just shrugs and says it's a weird night.

"You've changed." I say it with all the honest admiration I can muster. I like her. I like her bite, her snap, her strength.

She nods. "It's been a long time." Another short, spare statement. "Have you changed?"

I exhale roughly. There it is. My opening. "Yeah. A fair bit. I realized I'm an addict."

She looks immediately to the drinks between us.

I'm used to that. I don't shirk away from the unspoken question. "Not booze, although I don't drink a lot. I don't need another addiction in my life. But I don't like the stuff enough to use it in that way. No, I'm a gambler. I've been in recovery for almost four years."

Her eyes go wide. "Cards?"

And how. At university, my poker games were legendary. And they came first, before Regan, before sports, before anything I should have valued. "Cards, horses, money. I…" I gesture to my suit. "I don't actually do any of the investing part of being an investment banker anymore. Crashed and burned hard a couple of years ago. Got my brother in a shit-load of trouble. We came out the other side of that bruised but better. Now he manages the investment side of things, and I make house calls on our more eccentric clients who like that I'm a wild boy."

She laughs gently. "That makes you sound like a gigolo."

"Not far off," I say gruffly.

"Is that why you're going to Ottawa tonight?"

He nods. "We have a client there. I'll come home tomorrow morning."

"You're going up for one night?" Her eyes sparkle. "Are you literally a gigolo? No judgement."

I smile. "No, but I was going to spend the night with her." The look on Hazel's face is incredible. An almost impercep-tible flash of jealousy, which I enjoy, but then honest, naked curiosity. "Because she's a night owl. We usually have a late dinner, and then spend the night pouring over her accounts before having breakfast together. Sometimes we finish late in the night and I grab some sleep, other times it's an all-nighter until I head back to the train."

"Long round trip. Why don't you fly?"

I grimace. "I, uh, can't."

Her eyes go wide and her voice softens. "Phobia?"

"Insider trading."

Her mouth falls open and a small squeak comes out. "Huh."

"Yeah." I clear my throat. "It's not universal. I can get on planes. Just not the ones operated by the two companies I put in financial peril. In hindsight, it was dumb to piss off both domestic airlines like that." Then I grin, because I know it could be way worse. It had been, for a couple of years. It had been brutal, and a mess entirely of my own making. Now, my life was back on track. "It's an inconvenience, but I'm in no place to complain. I could be in jail and I'm not."

"That sounds like quite the story," she says, her eyes still wide. "I don't want to pry, though."

"Pry away. Part of the twelve steps is taking responsibility and coming to terms with what I did."

"So I've heard, but I've never seen it represented quite that honestly before." She pauses as the food cart rattles towards us.

"Festive turkey, salmon, or lasagna, miss?"

"Lasagna for me, please."

I take the same.

She looks at me curiously as we dig into our food.

"Ask your questions," I finally say.

"You're for real."

"It's not like you're a stranger," I say under my breath. "You knew me at my worst."

"That was your worst? And you ended up doing..." She licks her lips. "Something that got you banned from airplanes?"

"It was part of the agreement. It's almost done. I'll be able to fly to Ottawa next year, although I'm sure I'll have a hassle the first few times."

"You seem chill about that."

I laugh hollowly. "I've adjusted to the surreal nature of my predicament. And again, it's entirely of my own making."

"You added that caveat again."

I always do. I take a deep breath. "I ruined my life before it really got started. I don't want to make that same mistake. In general, I believe in ruthless honesty. It's humbling."

"But you didn't mind when I gave you a different name?"

No, I really hadn't. I was more curious than anything. "You had your reasons."

She hesitates.

"Didn't you?" I arch one eyebrow. I don't really care. She doesn't owe me anything.

Slowly, she smiles. "Ruthless honesty?"

"It's a good policy."

She licks her lips, the tip of her tongue pink and nimble. "Okay. So, the thing is, Aibhlin…that is my name now. In some ways. I'm a writer. It's a pen name."

"What do you write?"

"Words strung together in sentences. Lots of them."

I suppress a chuckle. "How mysterious."

"Mmm."

Her eyes are definitely sparkling now, so I take a gamble. "Were you enjoying our game until I ruined it?"

She purses her lips, then nods. "Yes."

"Damn. So was I." I think about her ice demon story.

"You're a good storyteller. I'd love to read something else that you've done. Anything."

Her cheeks turn pink. "Do you like dinosaur erotica?"

It's damn good I didn't put that bite of lasagna in my mouth before she said that, because it would have launched right back out.

"There's a first time for everything." I ignore the rough gravel in my voice suddenly.

"Oh, good." She blinks innocently.

"Do you—" I reach for my glass, wait a beat, and when she doesn't help me out, I swill back the last of my rye. "Uh, is that what you write?"

"No." She winks. "But I really enjoyed that exchange."

"All right, funny girl."

"There's nothing wrong with dinosaur porn, Sam."

"There's a difference between porn and erotica, Hazel."

She freezes. "Yes," she says slowly. "There is."

"Are we still joking around?"

"Yes." But she licks her lips. "No. I write erotica. That part was legit. No dinosaurs yet, or ice demons."

"That's a shame." My pulse jacks up at the thought of Hazel writing anything erotic.

Above our heads, the speaker crackles to life. "*Our apologies for the long wait, folks. Unfortunately, due to weather and other circumstances, we are returning to Toronto. We should be back in the city by ten o'clock. If Toronto is not home, and you need assistance for the night, please see the ticket agents in the station for accommodation options.*"

Hazel makes a sad face as the train begins to move back in the direction we came from. "Well, that's too bad."

I refresh my Twitter search. No update on the collision. "Yeah."

"Will you try to get on one of the trains tomorrow?"

I shake my head. I'm already emailing my client. "This meeting will be rescheduled to the new year. You?"

"I'm going on holiday, and have reservations I don't want to cancel, so I'll head out again in the morning. Hopefully the rooms they find us aren't too far away from the station."

My eyebrows shoot up. "You don't live in Toronto?"

She shakes her head. "Stratford."

I wouldn't have pictured her as settling in a small town. "Fascinating."

"Is it?" She laughs. "Why?"

"I don't know." I'm smiling now, too.

"Where did you think I'd ended up? Not that I'm assuming you thought of me."

"I did think of you. From time to time." My throat gets tight, thick, as I think about the reckless years after graduation. Luke's ascent to the pinnacle of Bay Street trading, our launch into our own boutique firm. I should have thought of Hazel more often. Remembered the derision she felt for me and taken a lesson from that, instead of learning it the hard way, after risking everything. "I don't know. I wondered what you were up to. I didn't think about where, though. In a lot of ways, I froze us in that moment."

"That night?" She breathes the two words, and heat crawls up the underside of my skin.

"Yeah."

She blinks slowly, and God damn it, I'd kill for us to be alone on this train right now. For there to be a dark nook somewhere we could replay that night, have another chance at a dirty kiss to test that still very-much-there sizzle. "What do you remember?"

My balls pull tight against my body as I drop my gaze to her mouth. "I remember wanting to talk. It was too loud, and everyone we knew was there, so you didn't want to get too close right there on the dance floor."

She licks her lips. "Do you remember what you wanted to talk about? I've been trying to figure that out. How that night started."

"Regan had started dating someone else," I said slowly. "And that was good. I was happy for her, but it was bitter-sweet because I'd fucked up and lost a good thing. Even if we weren't meant to be forever, I regretted not being a better boyfriend while we dated. So I was feeling sorry for myself, and her, and then you showed up. You were just...you. Sharp. Knowing. Challenging. I couldn't stay away. And I wanted to find out if you knew about Regan's new boyfriend, if you knew she had moved on. Which is, as I say that out loud right now, an incredibly immature set of thoughts. I know that, but there it is. Welcome to the mind of a twenty-one-year-old shithead."

"I didn't know, actually. Not until the next day." The words slide out like silk, soft and secret.

An unsettling thought burns in my mind. *Would it have made a difference?* But there's no point in retracing old ground.

"Without putting too fine a point on it, when I've thought of you over the years, it's always fondly as the one who got away." I smile. "And it's for the best that you did. It took me years to sort myself out."

"Really dodged a bullet?" She winks. "I've thought about you, too. Not as the one who got away."

"I imagine not." I say it dryly, but with affection.

"But that kiss…" Her voice drops to a sweet, husky note. "I've thought about that. Where it would have taken us. And never in all of those permutations did I guess at *this*." She spreads her hands wide.

"How many permutations?"

Another slow blink. Were her eyelashes always that luscious dark brown tinged with blonde tips? How stupid was I a decade ago that I never noticed? She smiles. "There were some elements of that evening that I've used over and over again in my stories. The way you…" She trails off and looks at my hands, then back up to my face.

And she blushes.

But I don't find out what it was—the way I *what?*—before the steward returns to collect our dinner trays.

Once we're alone again, she changes the subject. "Who have you kept in touch with from school?"

"There are people who stayed in the city and got into the business world. I see them from time to time. I stayed in touch with some of the guys until everything imploded. Did a few bachelor parties to Vegas, that sort of thing. But that's all in the past." Except for one person. "And I hadn't been keeping up with Regan, but I wrote to her last year. Part of making amends, the process of repentance, is an honest reckoning of the hurt I've caused. She wrote back and wished me well."

"She didn't tell me you'd reached out," Hazel murmurs. "We talk semi-frequently. Follow each other's lives online." She hesitates. "She's married. Did she tell you?"

"Yeah. Two kids. She seems happy. I'm glad."

Hazel nods. "She is happy."

"Does she know that we kissed, back in the day?"

Her eyes blaze. "Of course she does. I wouldn't have kept that from her."

No, of course not. My neck flushes and my gut twists in shame.

"I'll tell her about this, too." Hazel drags her lower lip between her teeth. "Although now I'm wondering why she didn't tell me you'd been in contact."

"Maybe for the same reason I wrote to her, and not to you? You were very clear with me that you didn't want to have anything to do with me."

She smiles ruefully. "True."

Then she wrinkles her nose.

"What?" I ask.

"This is all quite…weird. Don't you think?"

"Oh yeah, for sure. I'm a riot of intense emotions over here."

She laughs. "Stop it."

"Don't I look it?"

She drags her gaze over me. Takes her time, too, until I'm aching for more than her eyes. "No," she finally says, lifting her attention back to my face. "Although maybe I wasn't looking hard enough. What are you feeling right now?"

Nothing appropriate to say on a train, no matter how private our seats feel. "That I'd really like to continue this conversation when we get back to Toronto. You could—"

She shakes her head. "No."

"Hear me out. Then you can say no, and we'll go our separate ways if you really think that's best. The next time I see you—if I ever have the pleasure—I'll wait for you to introduce yourself, with whatever name you're using then."

She presses her lips together and waits.

I can't read the expression on her face, but I forge ahead anyway. "It's three days before the holidays. Like you said yourself, what kind of rooms are they going to find you? My place isn't far from Union. I have a spare room. You're welcome to stay with me tonight. And it would mean that our fun doesn't have to end just yet." I lean in. "I've enjoyed getting to know you again, Hazel. For what that's worth."

"A spare room?"

"If you want."

She turns her head to the side and looks out the window. "We're nearly there. I can see the lights of the city."

"The station is going to be a madhouse. Do you really want to stand in a chaotic line when I can offer you…" I do a mental cataloguing of my fridge contents. "Wine, water, and maybe tea, if my milk hasn't expired."

She doesn't answer right away. The announcement comes on overhead that we're five minutes away from Union Station.

By the time the train steams to a halt under the cavernous roof, I'm sure she's going to say no. My chest twists as she slowly gathers her belongings, then gives me a bittersweet smile.

"I'll walk you to the concourse," I say, putting off the goodbye a few more minutes.

She opens her mouth, but whatever she was going to say dies on her lips. She snaps her head in a quick, decisive nod. "Sounds good."

4

HAZEL

WE'RE the last ones off the train, and as soon as I step down onto the platform, Sam's beside me. He takes my carry-on suitcase and crosses it to his far side, letting our close arms brush as we walk together.

I can feel him even through our winter jackets. Me in my parka, him in a proper wool overcoat.

"So," I say after we walk up the ramp. There's a long line of people at the ticket counter. None of them look happy, and there's an angry buzz of conversations as hundreds of holiday plans get discussed and revised and ruined all at the same time.

"So," he repeats. "Look—"

"I should figure out what I need to do with my ticket." But I don't move.

I don't want to get in that line.

I don't want to say goodbye, because we've done this once

39

before. We've left unfinished business on the table for a decade, and it didn't feel good.

"Would you want to have sex?" I blurt out. That is not at all how I'd write it in a book. Nothing ever happens the way I write it in a book, though, so why should this be different? "If I came back to your place?"

He grins and shoves one hand through his perfect hair, making it even more perfect. "Want to? Hazel, I got one kiss ten years ago and I've always wanted more. I'm not going to pretend to be a Boy Scout. But whatever we do is up to you. We can just talk. Or maybe we could…" He drops his gaze to my mouth, and I can feel his lips there. The one kiss we shared. The reason I never wanted to talk to him, ever again. "Would you want to try another kiss?"

"Yes," I whisper. "Wait. No."

I look around. Not here.

Reaching out, I wrap my hand around his wrist and tug, leading him away from the main concourse and down a hallway past the business lounge.

It's not a dark nook at a club, but it's a bit more private.

I stop and turn in, closing the space between us. "Hi," I say, and my voice wavers a bit.

"Deja vu," he murmurs. "Are you okay?"

"It's been a long day and I was supposed to start a mini-break getaway for one, but instead I ran into a guy I once kissed, on the train, and then an ice demon stopped us in our tracks and now I think I'm going to kiss him again. It's all a bit overwhelm—" I swallow as he brushes his fingers against my cheek. "—ing," I add in a whisper.

"That's quite the day." He leans forward, his breath warm as our faces get closer to each other. "Are you going to kiss him, or do you want him to kiss you?"

I push up on my toes, giving him my mouth. His lips are warm and firm, yielding to my exploration. He feels like he's smiling, and I like that. I like it even more when he slides his hands into my hair.

Ten years has changed how he kisses. The setting is wildly different, too.

But I know this mouth. Not well. Just a fleeting, perfect memory. A bittersweet what-if remembrance that would pop up from time to time, and is now blooming once again in my mind.

A long time ago, when we were both different people, we'd wanted to sleep together and for very good reasons we chose not to. I chose not to, anyway.

Tonight, I want to make a different choice.

I lean back against the wall, finding an inch of space between us. Too much, but necessary for a conversation. "So, your offer…"

"Yes." Sam brace exhales hard, then braces his arm above my head and looks down at me with a kiss-drunk smile. "Tea, and uh, friendship. Spare room if you want it."

"I don't want the spare room. When I asked if you wanted to have sex, I meant, I want to have sex. With you."

He blinks down at me.

"Is that too forward?"

He swears under his breath and crushes me against the

wall in the gentlest way possible, his mouth hot and demanding against mine.

No. Not too forward for Sam Preston.

Excellent.

Eventually we stop kissing long enough for me to get in the (now shorter) ticket line. The ticketing agent explains they're trying to add another train on for the next day, but they can't say yet what time it will be at.

I'm definitely missing my afternoon check-in at the fancy Christmas lodge.

But I don't care.

When I return to Sam's side, he has good news. The collision on the train tracks has finally been confirmed by the provincial police, and it's a holiday miracle, because there were no fatalities.

This time, I kiss him right in the middle of the concourse. When we break apart, Sam takes the lead, guiding me outside. It's relatively quiet now, just a few pedestrians trudging through heavy sludge on Front Street. Snow has been falling steadily on the city for a while, blanketing it in a lovely silence.

He flags a waiting taxi and hustles me into the back. He gives an address I don't recognize, and when we head west, I realize why—Sam lives in an area that was nothing but old warehouses when we were in university. Now it's an in-fill village inside the city, with impossibly attractive townhomes on newly created streets, glittering restaurants, and retro-fitted lofts in the warehouses.

It's one of these we stop in front of.

Despite his legal troubles, Sam has done okay for himself.

He doesn't say anything until we're in the elevator. But when we're alone, he leans in and brushes his lips against my temple. "Did I make it clear that, while I gambled and lost a lot of money, I paid back all my debts? I spent two years living on my brother's couch. I moved here six months ago. I wouldn't seduce you back to my den of ill-gotten gains."

I tip my head to the side so I can see the edge of his profile. "I was wondering. A little."

"I'm an open book." His voice rubs against my skin. "About my mistakes, or anything else."

"Anything?"

His lips twist into a smile. "Ask your questions."

Instead, I confess a deep, dark secret. "I wanted you so much back then. It was awful, because I thought you were awful—"

"I was." He grins, and it makes my insides flip-flop.

"But I wanted you anyway. Actually, no, I wanted you because you were awful. That unrepentant bad boy appeal."

"Don't tell me you're disappointed to discover I've straightened myself out."

I laugh and turn more fully so I can look right at him, and so he can see my face. "Not at all. When I realized who was sitting across from me, I was...wary. The Sam I knew had a twisted appeal which my foolish twenty-one-year-old self was briefly into, but I wouldn't have come home with him."

"He didn't deserve you." He presses against me and brushes my hair away from the collar of my jacket. "But I can still be wicked."

"Good." I lick my dry lips. "I can be wicked, too."

"I have no doubt. Can I ask you something?"

It's only fair. "Yes."

"You started to tell me something on the train. It made you blush." His fingertips trail up my neck and onto my cheeks. "I like the way you blush. Would you tell me what that was? What do you remember from the night we kissed?"

My pulse pounds. "You circled my wrist with your fingers. It was—I mean, maybe you were just dragging me off the dance floor, but there was something about how you held my arm. It felt good."

He groans as the elevator comes to a stop. "And remembering that makes you blush?"

Heat swarms through me. "Yes. Definitely."

He cups my face and kisses me softly. "Good. Let's play with that."

I'm not any kind of innocent. I've spent the last ten years doing my best to navigate the dating swamp, but too often sex is a mediocre experience.

The good sex I've had has been amazing.

The bad sex, though—to call it off-putting would be a kindness. So I've learned to be straight up with my desires. Some guys get weird about that.

Not Sam. Not *this* Sam, anyway. Grown-up, owning his mistakes, and—as he opens the door to his apartment—coming out the other side of that with a *very* nice loft.

I whistle as I step over the threshold. It's ruthlessly empty, but not cold. There's an obscenely large couch in the middle of the space, covered in pillows and a generous throw blanket. Soft, touchable. But the dark plank floors between us and the sofa are completely bare. Beyond it, there's a television on the wall and a low, wide walnut bookshelf below that. That's it for the entire living space. Everywhere you look is an endless expanse of wood floor, leading to an open kitchen area at one end, and a set of doors at the other. Abstract art and sculpture decorate the space, making his loft more a gallery than a home. It takes my breath away.

"This is a nice place. You have a, wow, gorgeous art collection."

"It's almost all my sister-in-law's work, and the paintings she curated for me. It was a housewarming gift, because she was so glad to get me off her couch. I'd mooched far too long while I was feeling sorry for myself."

I shrug out of my coat, and he takes it. While he hangs it up, I move closer to a mixed-media sculpture of a woman. "Is she...masturbating?"

He laughs, then sighs. "Yes. Most of it has an erotic bent. That's Grace's thing. Woman-focused erotic art."

"I love it." I move to the next piece, a painting that's mostly atmospheric, and finally stop in front of a statue set into a nook on the wall. "I love all of it. She has great taste."

"She'll get a kick out of that compliment, and from a fellow creator, too."

I turn my head and smile at him. "I still haven't told you

my pen name. Maybe I made all of that up because of our ice demon story."

"Did you?"

I don't answer. "We started an interesting conversation in the elevator."

He's taken off his suit jacket as well as his overcoat, and I reach out, pressing my hands against the soft, white cotton shirt stretched across his broad chest. He's bigger now than in university. But he's also grown into his body.

"I wrote a poem about you once," I murmur as I trace the shape of his body.

He shudders. "There once was an asshole from Toronto?"

I burst out laughing. "No. It's nice. It's called…" I trail off and step back. He moves closer. I step back again, and we pace across the loft like that, him chasing me.

By the time we reach the floor-to-ceiling windows on the far side, my body is humming.

"Hazel," he growls. "Tell me."

"The sounds I imagine you make." I whisper as he cages me in against the cold glass. "A growly burr/A slow fade into exhalation/A groan/A gasp."

"I'll groan for you," he whispers as he unzips my hoodie.

I close my eyes as he finds the bare skin at my waist, then slides his hands underneath my t-shirt, against my belly. My ribs. Just shy of my breasts. "When I'm on my knees/Or above you, head curved low."

"Will you suck me? I'd like nothing more than to see my cock in your beautiful mouth."

I smile and keep going. "Beneath you, shifting/As you pin my arms against the bed."

He groans now, for real, and buries his face in my neck. Open-mouthed. Wet, hungry. He sucks on my skin as heat ratchets up between us. But I'm not done yet.

"I would love to wring your pleasure/In a thousand ways/As the sounds I imagine you make/Get me every time." I gasp when I finish. "Sam, please."

He lifts his head, his eyes dark and glittering. "Tell me that's in the poem. *Sam, please*. Nothing would make me happier. I'd die a king in my own mind."

I grin. "It's not, but I'll write it out for you that way if you make me come twice tonight."

"What do I get for the third and fourth orgasm?"

"I see you're still cocky in some regards."

"Only my commitment to your satisfaction, my sexy little poet." He kisses me again, deep and intensely, his tongue rough and perfect and then soft, which is perfect, too. "Turn around."

I spin in his arms, my hoodie being discarded in the process, and I gasp. The storm has picked up in a sudden flurry of white mess. We're up high enough we can see that flakes aren't just falling to the ground, but being pushed upwards by the wind as well. It's a rolling, angry fight of the elements.

"The ice demon's still not pleased," Sam murmurs in my ear. "What's wrong now?"

"Maybe he's not angry," I pant. "Maybe he's worked up. Excited."

Through his suit pants and my yoga pants, I can feel the thick length of Sam's cock. It twitches, a heavy push against the curve of my ass. He nips at the curve of my ear.

I'm pressed against the glass, and if it weren't snowing, someone on the street below would be able to see me. But right now, we're all alone up here. Lovers caught in the middle of a snow globe.

"Do you want to fuck me here, Sam? Up against the window?"

His teeth scrape against the nape of my neck. "I want to stretch you out on my bed and pin you down." He finds my arms and wraps his fingers around my wrists. "Unless you want it here."

I want his cock in my mouth first. I want to crawl around on top of him and taste him, make gasp. "Here. If you like."

"Oh, I like." He tightens his grip, but his thumbs stay soft and stroke up and down on my skin as he presses against me obscenely. "I want to consume you in every possible way. I want to crawl between your thighs and kiss you there, too. I want to taste your breasts, your belly, your back. Your ass. Every inch of you."

"Yes," I breathe.

It doesn't matter what we do. Not really. All of it will be right, because I can't pretend any longer.

As messed up as it is, Sam *is* the one who got away. And that's a good thing, but my body doesn't care. I'm back in university, about to do something reckless and crazy hot. A gorgeous, glorious mistake.

I tug against his tight grip on my wrists. He doesn't let go, and my thighs tremble all the way from my knees up to the slick, swollen space between them.

"Tell me, Hazel," he croons in my ear. My pussy floods with a fresh wave of arousal. "Tell me what you want it."

"Force me to my knees," I gasp. "Make me suck you."

5

SAM

BLOOD POUNDS IN MY EARS. In my cock. Deep in my belly, where nerves threaten to take over.

But tonight, what Hazel wants, Hazel gets. I drop my hands to her shoulders and spin her around.

"You want that?" I ask it as roughly as I just grabbed her. Hard, unyielding. As if this is a final chance to say no, but of course it's not. I'll be gentle with her, in spirit if not in body.

Her eyes are wide. But the corners of her mouth curl up in a slow, knowing smile as I slide one hand up the side of her neck, my thumb grazing her throat before I thrust my fingers into her hair and make a fist. "Yes," she breathes. "Do it."

I tug my hand down, leading her, and she bends, her legs folding as she drops to her knees.

"That's a good girl," I tell her, tugging on her hair so she has to look up at me. With my free hand, I cup the bulge jutting rudely at the front of my dress pants. "You want this?

You want to hear what it does to me for you to slide that pink, slick mouth along my cock?"

"Yes, please."

"So polite." I rock on my heels, brushing my fabric-covered cock against her face. "Take it out, Hazel. Play with me. Make me…what was it you wanted to hear? A groan?"

She nods eagerly as her fingers fumble with the zipper. I let go of her hair long enough to help her. I undo my belt, she does the rest, and as her fingers tug at the elastic of my briefs, my cock rises angrily between us. A thick, ruddy erection, already wet on the tip at the promise of her mouth.

Her lips part, her tongue peeks out, and then she swallows me. Head first, then a bit more. She bobs her head, taking a bit more with each sloppy suck, and when she pulls back, it's with enough suction I want to thrust my hips hard and bury myself deep in her throat.

I do more than groan, too. I hiss and growl, moan her name, and none of it is for effect. I've got a hand in her hair again, but not as tight this time. I'll be rough with her again soon enough. I'm going to haul her over my lap and give her *all* the fucking praise when she's done sucking my soul out of my body.

"Hazel." Her name is a broken plea on my lips. "I'm close."

She doubles down, swirling her tongue against the underneath of my cock. Milking me. That's the only way to describe it. I feel the orgasm start deep inside me, then my balls contract, pumping lewd spurts against the back of her mouth as she takes big, gulping swallows.

Oh, fucking hell. "Yes," I say, then suck in a big, gulping

breath. "Yes, God, yes. Hazel, that was fucking perfect. You beautiful woman. Come here."

I brace myself against the window and pull her hair gently now, encouraging her to rise. Up she gets, and I kiss her perfect, filthy mouth. Her glorious little tongue which still tastes of me, and her sweet, swollen lips which did some seriously hard work just now.

I do my pants up again, then pick her up in my arms and carry her to the couch.

"That was hot," I say once she's settled on my lap. I stroke the curve of her breast through her shirt. "Were those some of the sounds you imagined?"

She grins and wiggles in my lap. "Yes."

"As good as your fantasy?"

She groans. "You are so cocky. And yes, even better."

I throw a fist in the air, and she pushes at me, which makes me push back. Then tickle.

She squeals, and I slide my fingers higher under her shirt, cupping her breasts. "I want to see more of your skin."

She peels off her shirt, then her bra. I pull her closer, bringing my mouth to her nipples. First one, then the other. A scrape of my teeth, a hard swallow of her flesh, all the while pinching the other taut, brown tip.

Back and forth, until I'm drooling from the taste of her and she's grinding against me.

I flip her to the side, crawling on top of her. She wraps her legs around me, and I pin her down.

"You were such a good girl," I murmur between kisses. She whimpers in response. "And now it's your turn. I'm going to suck on your sweet little pussy now, Hazel. Can you hold very still for me?"

She squeaks as I move down her body. I catch her leggings at the waistband and pull them down, her panties coming with them. I strip her down to nothing in an instant, and I'm rewarded with a blush even prettier than the one on the train.

Hazel, nude and stretched out on my sofa, is a work of art more precious than anything on my walls.

I trace the shape of her with my fingertips.

"You're blushing," I tell her as my fingers wander up her neck and rub rudely against her lips.

She licks at my hand. "Am I?"

"Yes. And it makes me hard. You know what else makes me hard?"

She shakes her head, smiling. "Tell me."

"When I squeeze your skin, it turns the same pretty shade of pink. And now every time I think of you blushing, I'm going to remember..." I rake my hand down her torso and she gasps. "That sound. My God, it's perfect."

"Were you this dirty ten years ago?" Her eyes are wide, and she bites her lip.

"I don't think I was this dirty ten hours ago, Hazel. We have some smoking chemistry between us, though, so who knows what would have happened?" I lean over her and suck one of her nipples into my mouth with a wet, hungry slurp.

Fuck yes.

No more waiting.

I need to know what the most sensitive part of her tastes

like. I drop to the floor and drag her to the edge of the couch, pulling her outside leg over my shoulder.

Kissing my way up her inner thigh, I take a moment as I reach the crease between her leg and her pussy to breathe her in and appreciate the soft, gentle beauty of her body. Her curls are blonde here, lightly dusting the darker skin of her labia before giving way to the delicious pink of slick, wet skin inside her folds. I run my nose along the curls before tracing the same path with my fingers.

She shivers, but holds still, as I told her to. I lift my head long enough to praise her again, then bow back to my task.

The first taste of her is musky and light, the second stronger and sweeter. I lick up to her clit and then circle it, slowly at first, long licks, before closing my mouth around the hard, throbbing nub and sucking.

She comes up off the couch, her hands sliding into my hair, and croons my name. "Sam…"

Damn straight. I want her to say my name as she comes on my face. I want her to lose her mind while I suck her off, just as I lost *my* mind at the window.

I push her thighs wide with my forearms, opening up her cunt for my mouth. My fingers. My teeth, just to test, as I nip at her labia.

"God, yes," she cries out. "Sam, please."

"Tell me," I demand. "Tell me what you want."

"Fuck me."

"Condoms are all the way in the bedroom, babe. You gotta come first, then I'll drag you to my bed. Is that what you want?" I slide two fingers into her slick, tight hole. "That's right. Fuck my hand."

I dip my head again and capture her clit again as she bucks against my mouth.

Her climax is bold and fast, just like Hazel. She floods my tongue with a burst of sex and passion and something unique to this night, to this woman.

I bury my face in the soft, tender skin of her inner thigh when she pushes my head off her sensitive flesh. *This woman.* Who wanted me to push her to her knees, and is now stroking my hair.

It's not until after she starts to laugh that either of us remembers I told her to hold still.

"You could punish me," she says, giggling, as I strip out of my clothes. Once I'm naked, I haul her off the couch and shove her playfully toward my bedroom.

"I will absolutely spank you, the second I catch you," I growl.

She shrieks and runs ahead, but she stops as soon as she gets through the doorway. "Oh, this room is even nicer," she says. "That view is whoa."

I catch her around the waist and bury my face in her neck. She smells warm and womanly, and I can't get enough. "Caught you."

"You tricked me with the CN Tower outside your window."

"Whatever I need to do to gain the upper hand." I pick her up and spin us around, pointing her to the bed. "Get on your knees."

She does, then wiggles her hips at me, and I pounce. It's less of a spanking and more of a wrestling match, where I need to dig my fingers into the soft curve of her hips to hold her in place, and she likes that even more than the light swats I land on her bottom.

"I'm sorry," she whispers, her eyes dancing, when I finally pin her down. She's stretched out on her back and I'm between her legs. The wetness of her pussy is a crazy distraction against the throbbing length of my cock.

"No you aren't."

She shakes her head, giggling. "Not even a little."

"So if I want you to hold still, I'll need to make you?" I curve one eyebrow up in a menacing look, and her face goes serious.

"I guess so," she says mock-solemnly. "Oh. No."

Fuck, I need to be inside this woman. "Come here, you minx," I murmur, tangling my hand in her hair as I kiss her.

Her tongue, her breath, the hard scrape of her teeth as she sinks them into my lower lip—all of it is magic, and none of it is enough. More. I need more.

I take her with me as I roll to the side of the bed, and she giggles. I grab a condom, then two more. Just in case.

That's how I enter her for the first time, with both of us on our sides, facing each other. Time slows as my pulse jacks up. She wraps her top leg over my hip. I roll the latex down my shaft. Her fingers wrap around my slick length and she guides me into her as I pull her close.

The look on her face is unforgettable. Eyes wide, then wider again, and her lips part.

"Oh," she breathes, and I feel it too. An obscene stretch, because she's slick but still tight, her little pussy eager for me but not quite ready. But then her heat gives way and inch by inch she slides onto me, until I'm buried all the way. "Sam…"

We fuck like that, entwined on our sides. Outside the window, the snow still swirls, a white blanket cocooning us from the world. There's no rush, and we take it slower than I've ever made love before.

Each thrust is a complete moment. Hazel moves inside a tight circle of my arms like she's always been there. I give her my all, finding the depths of her reactions and pushing there until she cries out.

It's beautiful. She's beautiful, but the act itself feels like her poem. *She wrote me a God damn poem.* And then she gave it to me, in breathy little gasps, when I don't deserve such sweetness.

I told her exactly who I am.

She knows.

And she's still pulling me into her body, letting me love her.

It's beautiful, but it's raw, too. *Vulnerable.* Exposed.

She looks at me like she sees right to my soul, and that should scare me. I've had enough of being put on display for a lifetime. I've been picked apart and judged and found lacking in the worst way.

I'm a social pariah. A menace.

But Hazel's right here, letting me love her.

And she's smiling. "Sam…"

God, yes.

"You fuck like a god."

Fucking. Not loving. *Keep it real, Sam.* Our conversation on the train rockets through my mind. Neither of us are romantic. I can't confuse great sex—mind-blowing sex—with more complicated emotional attachment.

I roll onto my back, pulling her with me. "Ride me, Hazel."

Her eyes sparkle as she wiggles on top of me. "Make me, Sam."

I squeeze her hips, urging her up. Her eyes flash, and she pushes against me, my cock disappearing inside her again.

My brain stutters over how good it feels to be fully sheathed in her sweet, tight cunt. I force her up again, her gasping cry a gorgeous reward. She resists again, sliding her heat back over me. We play that game for a few more thrusts, then I take over, holding her place with a firm grip as I fuck her from below.

Hard, demanding thrusts. Take it, come for me, take it, be more perfect. A riot of sensations numb my thoughts as she begins to shake. My thumb finds her clit, giving her something to grind against as I drive up and into her on a final ruthless plunge.

And then she collapses, and I'm coming, I'm coming, deep inside her, and the thoughts rush back.

So perfect, so warm, so real.

Hazel.

OUR SECOND ROUND of sex starts in the shower.

It ends with a hard, fast screw on the floor three feet from the shower, with Hazel perched on my lap, my cock buried deep in her clutching pussy.

She presses her forehead against mine, and the damp tendrils of her hair curtain us in.

Another cocoon. Another safe space for me to lose myself in her.

To pretend I'm not stuck in a weird place in my life where I'm desperately grateful for all that I have—and hating it all the same.

"Come for me, Sam," she whispers, and I do. Hard, fast, blindingly.

After we clean up again, we crawl naked into my bed.

Outside, the snow has died down. I gesture to the dark sky and the distant glint of a star. "The ice demon doesn't seem upset now."

"He convinced his beloved to return to his fortress with him." She wriggles in my arms. "That is not a metaphor for anything."

A pain that feels a lot like regret spasms in my chest. "I wouldn't presume."

"It's just good storytelling."

"Very."

She's quiet for a moment, and I run my fingers through her hair. "Sam?"

Before I can answer, my phone vibrates on the night stand. It's the middle of the night.

She glances toward it. "Do you want to check that?"

No, I want to bury myself in her body and pretend my life

and all the complications that come with it don't exist. "I probably should."

"Go." She rolls away from me, flopping out in the middle of my bed. A naked goddess, a blast from the past, when I was still a fuck-up but in other ways, less complicated ways.

I grab the phone. It's a text message from Grace, and that awful regret in my chest twists tighter. I don't click into the message right away. I don't want to. Whatever Luke has done, if he's missing or they're fighting, I don't want to deal with it right now.

I glance back at Hazel. At her bare skin, her dark gaze, locked on my face. My stomach churns. "It's my sister-in-law."

She nods. "Do what you need to do."

I don't know what that is. I never have, not really. My brain will trick me into making all sorts of bad decisions. "My brother's an asshole."

Hazel's expression doesn't change.

I don't know why I'm telling her this now. My phone vibrates again. "I need to—"

"Sure. Go."

I glance down at the screen.

Message deleted by the sender

"I don't know what she wants." I scrub my hand over my face.

"Come back to bed," Hazel whispers. "Come here."

I want to. I want to so fucking much it hurts. But it's three days before Christmas, and if I don't deal with this right now, it's going to wreck the entire holidays. I shake my head. "I can't. You should get some sleep. I have to go."

"Sam—" She cuts herself off. Then she smiles. "Thanks for tonight."

I crawl on top of her. I don't know what to say right now, but I know what to do. I kiss the ever loving hell out of her. I pin her down until I make her gasp against my mouth, and then I swallow that sound so it's mine.

Hazel's little sounds are all mine now. "I'll be back," I whisper.

She curls up in my blankets, naked and perfectly bare as I pull on clothes I don't want to wear. I flip off the lights, hoping I'll return before dawn lights up the sky.

I don't make it.

And when I return, not only is my room lit with cool grey morning light, it's also empty. And Hazel has left me a *Dear Sam* letter on my pillow.

6

SAM

Four years earlier

I KNEW IT WAS COMING. My lawyers had warned me it would
be a possibility, although they would try to argue for a transi-
tion period.

The judge made it clear that would not be the case. She
didn't find any reason to grant me further compassion than
keeping my ass out of jail, and that was only because my assets
covered my debt to society—just barely, leaving me eight
hundred dollars to my name.

More than some had, she pointed out.

So I handed over the keys to my home and my cars, and
left the courthouse with my brother and sister-in-law.

Grace drove. Luke and I walked over from our lawyers'
office. We walk silently to the parking garage where she
parked.

"I'll find a place to stay," I say when we stop next to her car.

"Good," Luke barks.

Grace rolls her eyes at him. "He can stay with us as long as he needs to."

Luke shoots me a look that says it's over his dead body. If I had anywhere else to go, I'd leave right now. Give him space. He doesn't want me around. I've fucked everything up.

I open my mouth and nothing comes out.

I don't have anywhere to really go. That was bravado, and it turns out, I don't have any more of that to draw on.

Grace shakes her head. "You are staying with us. That's final."

Luke jerks his head back in the direction of Bay Street. "I'm going to the office. Someone has to start planning our next steps."

And it's not going to be the guy who's legally not allowed anywhere near the office. Fuck.

She shrugs. "Will you be home for dinner?"

"Yeah." He frowns. "I'll try."

She unlocks the Jeep and gestures for me to get in as he disappears into the stairwell.

I don't blame him for being mad. I'm not the only one who lost a lot of money today. All of our joint assets disappeared in the judge's sentencing. What assets he has left are Grace's, from her nascent art career.

She's done well for herself—really well.

It's still nothing compared to what we had.

Shoring up client accounts will consume his week now. *Fuck.*

We're blessed with light traffic, and it doesn't take that

long to get to their loft. It still has that new home smell. They sold their house in Forest Hill as soon as I was charged, back when Luke was speaking to me.

Back when he would spend any money to clear my name, until he realized there was no clearing of anything.

I was guilty of insider trading, guilty of gambling with every penny I could get my hands on.

He had sold the house he wanted to build a family in, moved into a soulless factory space as he called it, all for nought. His fuck-up of a brother had ruined everything.

Grace liked their new place, though.

That was some small silver lining. It was walking distance to her studio at the Waterfront Centre, close to the galleries and artsy shops she liked.

What did it fucking matter where Luke lived, anyway? He didn't do anything other than work.

Jealous.

Yes, I am. That was me, too, and now I have nothing. I don't have a loft, a beautiful wife, or a job.

I have a spare room with a view of a high-rise building and nothing but time on my hands to contemplate what a fuck-up I am.

"Do you want to talk?" Grace asks when we walk into the loft.

"No."

She brings me a cup of tea ten minutes later, anyway. She sets it on the bedside table and curls up next to me on the too-small bed. "Do you mind if I talk at you?"

I smile faintly. "No."

"You and Luke are a lot alike."

I growl, and she laughs.

"God, you're *so* alike."

I twist my head and look at her. Her face is soft, faint lines decorating her wide mouth and her tired eyes. She's beautiful and kind, and my brother doesn't deserve her. "What do you see in him?"

Her eyes go soft and sad at the same time. "I love him. I always have."

"He's an asshole."

"So are you, and I love you, too. So shut up and listen to me, okay?"

I make a face.

"It's time to talk to someone."

"I've spent the last year talking to people. Lawyers, mediators."

"A therapist. A real one, who can do trauma therapy around your childhood."

That makes me snort. We were raised in wealth and privilege, as I was sharply reminded by the judge today. So much wealth and privilege I got to keep my fucked-up ass out of jail because I could buy my way out of it.

Grace doesn't take the bait. She lets me laugh, then waits out my silence.

"No," I finally said. "I don't need a shrink. End of story."

It's not the end of anything, of course. She lets it go, but picks it back up again a few days later. Then a week goes by. Another poke.

I stop shaving, and she tells me even mountain men need to talk about their feelings.

But it's one day when I wander into her studio with takeout coffee that she finally says it another way.

"I think you were abused. Both you and Luke. And nothing will get better until you deal with it."

I don't know what I expected her to say, but it wasn't that. "Fuck no. Nobody ever hit me."

Her gaze doesn't waver. "There's more than one kind of abuse. Were you ever told you were loved? Ever hugged?"

The corners of her mouth curl down. "No." She sighs. "I'm sorry for the little boy who didn't get hugged enough."

Enough? Try at all. Fuck. A roaring, tearing ball of rage surges inside me.

Don't ignore me.

"You need to talk to someone."

"I'm talking to you."

"I'm not the right person to help."

"Grace, I know you mean well, but believe me—nobody else but you will ever see me as any kind of victim here. Part of my restitution to society is explicitly not framing myself in that light, all right? Leave it be."

But she's put something in my head, and it scratches at me. A burr.

Another week goes by, and I shave, because beards are

fucking itchy, but that's not the problem. The burr is inside. Grace put it there.

"Do you go to therapy?" I ask her one day after she has a fight with Luke about the fact that I'm in their space all the fucking time.

I'm aware, asshole.

"Not yet. I keep meaning to make some calls, but then I put it off. After my next show, after my next trip abroad. Later, next… you get the idea."

"It's hard."

She nods. "Want to make a deal? We'll both make appointments?"

I want to say yes, but I'm a liar. A no-good, manipulative jerk. I'm not sure I can say yes and mean it.

Grace can't see that about me, though. She gives me the sweetest, most earnest look. "We'll fix our brains together."

I round the kitchen island and squish her into a bear hug.

"I don't deserve you," I rasp into her hair. "I'll never not be there for you."

She wriggles free and shoves at my chest. She's tiny, and I don't go anywhere. "Oh God, I hope that's not true. I hope you get through this and move on with your life and get far too busy to even worry about me."

"That wouldn't be fair, not after all you've done."

"Life isn't fair, Sam. If it was…" She trails off.

I know.

If life were fair, everything would be different.

The next day, I go to my first Gambler's Anonymous meeting.

7

HAZEL

Present Day

I'M NEARLY at the front of the ticketing line when I see Sam burst through the front doors of the station. He ignores the fact there is a clear queue and storms right up to me. "So that's it?"

I glance at the person behind me, who makes no effort to pretend not to be curious about this early morning drama.

"You left," he says loudly, waving my letter in the air. It's pretty crumpled now.

Everyone else in line perks up as well.

"You left first." I shrug.

He glares at me like that's not fair.

It's all I want to give him, but he's under my skin whether I like it or not. I sigh. "And then I got an alert on my phone that they'd added another train today. I might make it to my hotel tonight after all."

68

He lifts his other hand in the air. It's clenched around his phone. "I got the same alert. Remember, funny girl? I had a ticket, too."

Oh. Well, that makes the contents of the letter a little more awkward. "You missed your meeting in Ottawa. Why would you…"

"*We* have unfinished business."

"We finished it last night. A few times, in fact." That gets a murmur out of the crowd. There, I've given them their thrill for the morning.

The line shuffles forward. So I shuffle forward, and Sam moves with me. He looks like he hasn't slept at all, because he spent the first half of the night having three rounds of sex with me, and the second half managing family drama. I don't want any part of the latter, but oh, the first part was very good.

I prefer him like this versus the polished man who sat down across from me last night. Now he's rumpled, and a little desperate. But I'd like him even more if he wasn't carrying a ton of baggage and family drama.

This line isn't the place to talk about that, though.

Or our unfinished business which he ominously brought up, but then didn't elaborate on. I bet our audience is disappointed that he's now just standing beside me silently.

When we reach the counter, I tell the ticket person my name and ticket number from yesterday. Sam leans in and does the same, as if we are together.

"We aren't together," I clarify.

"We bought our tickets separately, but we sat together

yesterday," he says, which isn't a lie. The clear allusion to us having some sort of romantic something on the train works on the ticket agent, too, who gives Sam a sweet, beaming grin. "If there's a way—"

But his charm doesn't help. She shakes her head after consulting with the computer. "I'm sorry, there aren't any more business class seats on this train. We can offer you economy seats and a partial credit for future use."

Economy is just fine by me. Less intimate than business class. And Sam won't cram himself onto a crowded train.

"That's fine," he says.

It's not. I swivel my head back and forth between him and the clerk, trying to find the right words to tell him to go home, but the way she's frowning at her screen and clicking furiously, I'm starting to get worried.

And then a sigh as the radio beside her crackles to life. The ticket person puts on her most sympathetic face. I'm not sure if she's more sorry about inconveniencing my plans or ruining Sam's clear attempts to train romance. "I'm so sorry."

I can feel my train ticket slipping away.

I'm ready for it when she says there is a problem with one of the cars, and no more tickets can be issued for this train.

I'm *fine*.

The hot prickle of tears behind my eyelids are simply understandable frustration. Nodding, I move away from the counter. And I take a deep breath, ignoring the rioting feelings inside me that are definitely about missing yet another trip and not about the too-large, too-confident presence right beside me.

Sam leans in, his voice low and sure. "I can get a car. I'll drive you to Ottawa."

Five hours in a car with the man whose bed I just slipped out of without so much as a goodbye. That won't be awkward at all. "Neither of us got much sleep last night. I was going to catch some rest on the train."

"Then we go back to my place and have a nap first."

"Sam—"

He catches me by the elbow and spins me around so we're glaring at each other. "Why'd you leave, Hazel?"

I look away.

"Don't do that," he whispers.

"I'm not doing anything."

"The cold shoulder of indifference is a Hazel McLaughlin classic," he bites out. "Don't *ignore* me."

Shock ripples through me. There's nothing confident about the hurt in his voice. As soon as he says it, he tries to take it back.

"I shouldn't—"

"Why would you say that to me?" But I know. I know the bark isn't about *me*, but I left his bed. *He left first.*

"I want more time with you."

"I'm not sure I do."

"Let me fix this."

"Is it something to fix?"

He has the good grace to at least look chagrined. "I don't know, but I hope so."

"What we have is a single night of sex and a decade of baggage. How do you fix that?"

An unexpected grin flits across his face. "A decade of sex."

"Sam!"

"It's basic math. We need balance."

I would never survive a decade of this.

"You're too much for me," I admit. The lack of sleep has made me painfully honest.

His jaw twitches. "I shouldn't have gone out last night."

He doesn't owe me an apology, but I notice that isn't one. It's a calculation of error.

I shake my head. "I would have found a way to say goodbye this morning either way."

He searches my face, his gaze hard, sharp. "I thought we had a connection."

We always will. That's the problem. "It was the storm. We got carried away."

"So what's your plan now? Find a bench to sit on?" He gestures at the cavernous main hall of the station. "Wait here until you can get a seat? Is that so much better than spending a few more hours with me?"

My chest aches because of course not.

"My life is a series of very bad decisions, Hazel." He leans in, his voice low and urgent now. "And the thing is, I've always known it. Every single time. I've known in the moment that it was a mistake to… Pick whatever fuck-up you want. Abandon my girlfriend for poker games. Bet every last penny I had and then some. Lust after my ex's best friend." A hard, bitter smile curves at his mouth. "But only because she didn't want me in the same way."

I did, though.

"Go into business with my brother. Get addicted to the wins. Forge relationships with people who could give me unfair advantages. Every turn. Mistakes I saw clear as day and embraced anyway."

"Last night," I whisper.

"Not a fucking mistake."

"For you."

"Ah." He laughs under his breath. "Well, I can't argue with that. I'm no good for you."

"That's…" I trail off. "Don't say that."

"It has to be what you're thinking."

"I just don't want to be pulled under. But I don't regret last night, at all. It was very good for me."

"I have some utility?"

"More than some."

"What if I make you a promise? No expectations. Nobody gets pulled under. You have an out whenever you want it, but let me get you to Ottawa first."

"Why?"

"Because I lost five hours last night. Because I lost a night a decade ago, that could have turned into something. Because of that decade of baggage. Maybe you won't give me a decade to fix it, but let me try to do *something*."

I laugh. "You just promised no expectations."

"I asked you if it would help if I did. You didn't take me up on it."

Letting go of my suitcase, I shove at his chest and he catches my hands, hauling me against him as I gasp his name in protest.

"Would it help?" he whispers against my mouth.

"I don't know."

He kisses me, hard, and I crawl up his body, winding my arms around his neck. This is a mistake, but it's a mistake that tastes good. And it feels good, too, which makes it the most dangerous kind of mistake—where I could forget it will end badly.

But one night wasn't enough. Maybe three more nights will quench my thirst for all things Sam.

AFTER A FEW MORE HOURS OF sleep at his place, and a restorative hot shower—which I make in peace, while he makes some calls in search of a car—we walk to his favourite breakfast place for a late brunch. By the time we're done eating, a friend of his arrives.

He shakes Sam's hand, then turns to me. "Alex Acosta."

The name niggles at me. It takes me three spins through the mental Rolodex. He writes young adult fiction, and his second book rode the bestseller list for a few weeks. "The novelist?"

"Busted." He grins and turns back to Sam. "You have excellent taste in friends." When he turns back to me, he leans in. "Nobody ever recognizes me, except maybe other writers."

Sam howls, and I turn pink. "Well..."

"What?" Alex grins even wider. "Are you a writer, too? Sam didn't say."

"Sam doesn't really know," I tell him. "Not really. I haven't told him my pen name. We're old friends from university, and we reconnected last night on the train to nowhere. It's a long story. Anyway, the short version is I'm an erotica writer, mostly. Nothing you'd have read."

"Don't assume that." He bites his lip, and if I wasn't head-over-something for Sam, I'd be all over Alex. He's adorable in a stern silver fox kind of way. "I shouldn't say that, of course."

"Your secret is safe with me."

"And yours would be safe with me," he says, winking.

"Maybe I'll tell Sam my pen name for Christmas, and he can share it then."

Alex laughs at that, then hands Sam a set of keys. "She's parked out front. Be gentle on her."

"I will."

"Will I see you on Christmas Eve?"

"Nah, won't be back until the twenty-fifth, right?" Sam looks at me.

I nod.

"So I'll make fun of your brother all on my own, then."

"Best of luck to you," Sam says gruffly. "But if he's an asshole, just give him space, okay?"

Alex waves him off, and I notice that Sam doesn't say anything about the middle of the night ride to his sister-in-law's rescue.

When we're alone again, Sam reaches across the booth and rubs his index finger against mine. "You don't need to share your pen name if you don't want to."

"It's not really a secret. I just didn't want you to Google me the way you searched up the train stoppage so quickly."

He groaned. "Damn, I showed my hand, eh?"

"You like to know everything. You always did. I liked the idea of keeping you off-centre. But you know the first part of my pen name, anyway, and if you remember any parts of the poem..."

"Is that published?" His eyebrows soar. "Wow."

I roll my eyes. "Your name isn't in it, remember."

"I meant I was impressed." His face shows it, too.

I soften. "Thank you."

"Shall we go back and grab our bags, and then hit the road?"

"Sure."

ALEX'S LUXURY Land Rover is nicer than any car I've ever been in.

I smooth my hands over the leather interior as Sam navigates onto the QEW heading east. "This is quite the car to just lend to a friend."

"Alex knows I'll be good to her. And he's not a materialistic kind of guy. Not anymore." When I look at Sam curiously, he shrugs. "We all have our demons. And some of us learn to look them straight in the face and tell them to get fucked."

"I like that." I think about my own demons. Of feeling stuck and frustrated. It might feel good to suggest politely that some things I'm hanging on to could take a flying leap.

"Easier said than done, of course." He signals for the exit to the Don Valley Parkway, then continues. "Did you ever meet my brother? He was on campus when we were doing our undergrads. He was at the biz school."

"I don't think so."

"We used to be really close." He frowns, his profile taut. "We haven't been for a long time."

"Alex is a friend of his, too?"

"Yeah."

I rake my teeth against my lower lip. He brought the topic up. "Alex doesn't know about the problems with Grace?"

"Nobody does. I wouldn't, if I hadn't lived with them." He swallows hard, his Adam's apple bobbing, then shoots me a swift look. "It's complicated, and private."

"I gathered. So…they have a Christmas Eve party?"

"Grace goes all out. It's quite glitzy. I used to like it, but I used to have questionable taste in everything, so…I dunno. Last year wasn't as much fun, and now… It's almost guaranteed we'd get into a fight at some point, and I'm over that."

"You and your brother?"

He nods.

"Don't you work together?"

"Yeah." He shakes his head. "And that can't last forever. It won't. I need another year to get back on my feet, and he needs time to build equity again, and then he'll buy me out of the firm. Or maybe I'll just walk away from it."

"That does sound complicated."

"It is." Another shake. "Not a festive topic, sorry. Let's discuss how you're going to tell me your pen name for Christmas."

I laugh. "Did you like that?"

"I loved it."

Before I left home yesterday morning, I packed one of my books to leave in the library at the lodge. Now I'm pretty sure I'm going to give it to Sam instead. The thought of what that would reveal makes my insides quiver, but it's not the worst feeling in the world. Not at all.

He reaches across the console and takes my hand. "Tell me more about this hotel that we're going to."

I recite the amenities and entertainment list by heart. "It's a big, gothic log cabin. A cross between a luxury hotel and a rustic lodge, with a three-storey fireplace that everyone gathers around for Christmas carols and fancy drinks."

"It sounds like something out of another time."

"That's the hope."

The rest of the five-hour drive to the Quebec border passes quickly, a blur of *"Do you remember this person from university?"* and *"I can't believe you've never watched that show"* and a lot of sidelong glances that make me feel toasty warm inside.

We arrive at the lodge mid-afternoon, exactly in time for the check-in I would have missed if I'd had to reschedule my train ride.

Sam pulls up to the portico and hands the keys to the valet. As we head inside, I realize his borrowed vehicle—and probably everything about him, including his expensive haircut—is more suited to this space than I could have guessed.

This is definitely more luxury hotel than remote lodge. And yet there is still that intensely gothic feel to it.

"Quite appropriate for an ice demon's fortress, don't you think?" Sam murmurs in my ear.

He's not wrong.

And that one simple question gets me all heated up again and distracts me through check-in. Our shared fantasy continues, now in a real-life movie-set quality setting.

Our room is every bit as stunning as the first impression of the entrance and lobby. Dark wood beams, a king-sized bed covered in crisp white linens and the softest wool plaid blanket I've ever seen in my life. The window is framed in matching plaid, and outside the sun is shining off endless fields of white.

"This is better than dealing with an asshole brother," Sam murmurs as he pulls me onto the bed.

"And way better than working over the holidays," I whisper back. "What do you want to do first?"

Sam licks the corner of my mouth, then moves down my neck. "You. Tell me more about our ice demon."

My pulse flutters under his attention. "What do you want to know?"

"What's the attraction for our heroine?"

I know what he's asking. What do I like about that particular fantasy? I close my eyes and think about it. A larger-than-life demon, furious and possessive. In real life, he's a jerk. Within the safety of an idea I entirely control—and can twist in any direction—it's delicious.

"Lots of things. His fury. His fear. That reaction. It's not safe outside of a story, but that kind of all-consuming passion..." I trail off.

He pulls back a bit. His eyes are dark, searching. "Hazel, you still with me?"

I blink up at Sam. "Yes," I breathe. "I'm with you."

"Where'd you go?"

I kiss him softly. "I was thinking about how scared I was."

"And now?"

"Now," I whisper against his lips as I move in again. "I don't want you to stop until we're both exhausted."

8

SAM

After sex, and before dinner, we go snowshoeing, which Hazel is very good at and I am not at all. She has the time of her life, and that's all that matters.

Dinner spills into drinks in the lobby. There's a huge stone fireplace in the centre of the room, and Hazel looks like she's been transported to a magical fairytale land.

When I return from the bar with our second round, Hazel is typing furiously on her phone. She holds up her index finger, then finishes her thought.

She's blushing when she looks up and thanks me for the drink, which makes me curious. "What were you just writing that made your cheeks go pink like that?"

The blush deepens. "A story idea."

"Can I ask about it?"

Her eyes go wide, the pulse at the base of her neck fluttering like mad, but she finally nods. Leaning closer, she shows me the screen of her phone. "I know I said I didn't want to work over the holidays, but sometimes these things just come to me."

It's a cryptic list of bullet-point ideas.

A castle
A central fireplace
Ropes holding up tapestries
A captive woman bound against the tapestry with those same ropes
The ropes have a mind of their own? Controlled by a demon?
Feels like being held down by many people. Do the ropes wriggle against her, like they're aroused, too?

As I read the list, my cock thickens, lengthens, and I shift in my chair, but I'm beyond finding a more comfortable position now. Where the hell does her mind come up with these things? And how am I supposed to get her back to the room and stretched out on the bed beneath me without anyone noticing I'm practically turning into the ice demon myself?

"Sam?" My name is a breathless question. *Do you like it?*

"You are...utterly surprising. And remarkable." I swallow hard around the thick block in my throat. "You got all that from just sitting here?"

"It's what I do."

"Amazing." And because I'm sure I'm about to become her number one fan, I need to ask. "Do you need to write more? Can I get you your computer?"

She giggles. "No, just getting the idea down for now is

enough. It might percolate in the back of my mind for months, or years. I might not ever write it."

"You need to write that." I'm not ashamed of the urgency in my voice. Fuck, that idea is a gift to the world. Or at least to me. "Do you ever tell stories out loud? Maybe for an audience of one? I could be a patron of the arts."

I love the way she laughs. I like the way she sighs and looks me straight in the eye even more. "I don't need a patron, Sam. Just to be clear."

"You do okay?"

A confident, secret smile is the only response.

Hazel has more than a decade of very good reasons to keep her cards close to her chest, I don't blame her, but the intimacy we have during sex—searing, raw reveals, every single time—has my head spinning a bit.

How far can I push her?

I don't want to find the line. Don't want to do anything that will ruin these few days she's granted me.

I have until Christmas Day to figure out how to show her I'm a changed man, worthy of a second—third, fourth fifth —chance.

9

HAZEL

THE NEXT DAY is more of the same. Sex, friendship, re-connection. Good food, great wine, and Christmas cheer. We even play Scrabble next to the giant fireplace, and Sam comes very close to kicking my ass.

"*Mizzly* is not a word," I say as he uses five of his last seven letters—including a blank he saved to the very end—to build that off my just-played *quiz*.

"Are you challenging?"

"God no. I can do math as well as you can re-arrange letters. I'm ahead by just enough points that you can have that momentary victory."

He leans across the table. "And what did we settle on for victor's spoils?"

I close the gap between us and bring my lips to his ear. "Loser licks first."

Sam squeezes the back of my neck, re-adjusting our head positions so he can have a turn whispering perfectly inappropriate things to me. "That's right. So please, Hazel, kick my ass. I want to pinch my way down to your soft, sweet, succulent pussy and feast on it while you scream my name."

From the next table over, someone clears their throat. My face heats up, but Sam doesn't miss a beat. "Yes?"

"We noticed you two had quite the rousing game of Scrabble there." *Rousing?* I do my best to bury the filthy image Sam put in my mind, and turn my head to see who Sam's new friend is.

It's a woman about our age, wearing a Fair Isle holiday sweater. A man in a matching sweater approaches carrying two mugs of steaming something. Apple cider, I realize as he sits down.

I hope they also play loser licks first, but in a wholesome way.

The woman beams at Sam. Perhaps she likes his perfect hair, too. And that's okay, I can share his hair. "If you're finished, we'd love for you to join us. We could play a game of cards?"

I wince. We haven't talked about his gambling again, but that doesn't sound like a good idea.

Sam doesn't miss a beat. "We have an appointment, unfortunately," he says smoothly. "But thank you for the offer."

We play the last few turns, each of us using one letter at a time.

I win.

We quickly put our game away, then beeline as if we actually do have an important meeting. Sam doesn't say anything about the card-game offer, but his grip on my hand is extra-firm, and his jaw is set in a way that makes me want to kiss it soft—but also, maybe, ask him to take me over his knee so he can turn my ass pink.

My bottom volunteers as tribute.

When we get up to the room, he pushes me up against the door, drops to his knees, and finds the bare slice of skin between the top of my jeans and the hem of my shirt. His tongue is a hot flame on my body, a lick of fire to which I immediately surrender myself.

His hands are rough against my thighs, shoving my legs wide. I brace my hands against the door behind me as I realize he's going to yank off my boots.

Do it, Sam. Take me.

He doesn't say a word. Just ruthlessly undresses me in hard, jerking motions that make me slippery wet.

Sam Preston is magic. Hard and soft at the same time. Rough and then, when I'm aching and ready for it, whisper soft with his tongue against my clit.

This is more than I ever thought possible. It's worse than I ever feared, back in the day. Sam is dangerous tempting. I knew it then. I pushed him away for exactly that reason. Because in one kiss I knew that if I had another—just one more—I'd be hooked enough to do something stupid like fall for him.

Then I went and kissed him again. Again and again, for two days. It took a decade, but I forgot just how dangerous Sam is for my heart.

And still.

And *still.*

I don't care.

He can consume me. Burn me up.

It'll be worth it.

What's the worst that could happen?

His hand reaches up blindly and presses me hard against the door. The wind rushes out of me as he loops my left leg over his shoulder and pushes up, tilting my hips out and away from the door—and right against his ravishing mouth.

This is the worst that could happen. Sam and his knowing smile. His complicated past and my better judgement—totally absent from the moment our train came to an unexpected stop.

And still my clit throbs in his mouth.

My pussy runs slick and hot for him.

Because the worst is better than I've ever had before, and I want more, whatever the cost.

FOR THE NEXT TWENTY-FOUR HOURS, I wrestle with how to frame the conversation to Sam. By the Common Law of Date Definitions, we're only on our second date. The first was deciding to go back to his place. Second was me inviting him on this trip. Maybe breakfast in between could be called a date, too, but even by the Pedantic Law of Date Definitions, we're on our third.

Fourth, if you count our kiss ten years ago.

Do angry kisses count as dates? The jury's still out on that.

"What are you thinking about?" Sam asks, bopping me on the nose lightly with his fingertip.

I shake my head to clear the cobwebs and blink up at him. I'd taken a seat near the fireplace and gone into la-la land while he went to the bar.

Now he's brought us very grown-up mugs of hot chocolate. I pick up one of the cups he sets in front of me, take a sip, and make an appreciative sound. "Thank you. I was, uh, counting how many dates we've had."

"Seven," he says without hesitation.

I laugh. "How do you count that many?"

Sam gives me an inscrutable look, then gestures for me to stand up. "Come on."

Curious, I let him lead me to a more private nook on the second-floor balcony that overlooked the fireplace. "What?"

He draws me close and takes my hot chocolate, setting it on the rustic table next to the couch we've got all to ourselves.

Then he holds up his index finger to begin the list. "Our first was a month after Regan and I broke up, and you definitely thought it was a study session, not a date. But I bought you coffee and walked you home. Technically a date framework."

My mouth drops open. He'd been going to the coffee shop anyway, for one thing, and for the other, we'd been heading in the same direction.

Technically, that's some imaginative framework. And it makes me feel funny inside.

He leans in, kisses my bottom lip, and nudges my jaw back up. "The second date was the reverse, a month later. You sought me out and I didn't realize until later because you were quite clever about it."

"I did no such thing," I protest.

"Library stacks, fifth floor. It was a Thursday night. You found me in a study room and suggested we study together."

"That's really not a date," I say slowly. But now I remember the night clearly. I did seek him out. "How did you know I was looking for you?"

"I didn't. Not then. Not until the night we kissed, and you told me to pretend I don't know you if I ever see you again. And you also said..." He gives me a sheepish look. "'*Or if I'm stupid enough to pretend I need a study buddy when really I want a —*' And then you cut yourself off, told yourself this was all fucking stupid, and you stormed off. I played that line over and over again in my head, and realized what it meant a few days later."

My mouth drops open for the second time. Because I remember it now. Exactly as he's described it. I'd been so shaken, so angry at myself for not realizing what I was doing, putting myself in his path when I'd wanted him for so long.

I'd wanted him for so long.

All the blood drains from my face. Ah, damn it all to hell.

"Hazel?" Sam swears under his breath and pulls me in close.

"I wanted you," I whisper over my pounding heart. "When you were Regan's boyfriend. I wanted you then. I didn't know. I swear, I didn't know."

He growls lightly in my ear. "That was ten years ago, Hazel. It doesn't matter now."

I know he's right. But I've never consciously acknowledged this before. I need a minute to realize just how much guilt I've been carrying in a locked part of my heart.

I wasn't honest back then. Not with myself, not with my best friend, and not with the man who, once single, put himself in my path again and again because he knew I wanted him there.

There's nothing I can do about the past.

But the present is entirely within my control.

I take a hard-fought deep breath and breathe in Sam's now very familiar scent. "So I really ruined our third date, huh?"

"It was pretty rocky, yeah." He kisses my temple. "Took me a decade to get a fourth one, and I needed an ice demon's help."

"You're counting the train as our fourth date," I whisper.

"From the second you introduced yourself as Aibhlin. You engaged me in a flirtatious role-play."

"Your place is date five, breakfast is date six, and this trip is date seven." I don't know what to say next. "Sam…"

"Seven dates is plenty, Hazel." My heart slams against my chest. I'd once imagined Sam saying something along those lines—*one date is enough, Hazel*—but not like this. Not this softly, or sweetly. Not this lovingly. "I will grant you a fair amount of *who-knows-how-we'll-end-up* doubt over the first three dates, because they weren't really dates, not in the proper way. I was young and stupid and lacked sufficient hubris to be your partner. But I knew on date four. I knew on the train that I wouldn't want to say goodbye again."

My chest is tight. My skin is tight. My mouth is dry.

But my heart. Oh, my heart. It's so soft right now, so squishy. "What are you saying, Sam?"

His fingers wrap around mine, and his gaze stays locked on my face. "It turns out, I've missed you all these years. I've had quite the rocky ride, and I'm damn glad you weren't around for that. I needed to go through all of that mess on my own and come out the other side of it a man who might just be worthy of you. I'm saying I want an eighth date. A ninth and a tenth, and then I want to just start seeing you all the time. I'll come to Stratford. We can meet on the train. If you have any reason to come to the city—"

I cut him off with my mouth, with my hands tight around his. A squeeze. A *don't-ever-let-go* kind of grab, and he takes the hint. His arms wrap all the way around me now, sweeping me into an epic hug where I end up sprawled in his lap and it feels perfect. He's warm and lovely, and beneath my bottom, he's growing hard.

"Yes, I'll go on at least three more dates with you," I whisper against the skin on his neck.

Then I lick him.

Because seven dates were plenty for me, too.

10

SAM

I WOULD HAVE SAID that Christmas Eve peaked mid-afternoon, when Hazel and I confessed just how long we've wanted each other.

But then the day gets better, and better, and better.

It's our last night in this winter wonderland. We're checking out in the morning, heading back to the city.

Back to reality.

And maybe it's because this is going to end that each moment feels sweeter than the last. Fucking magical, if I'm being honest.

When it comes to Hazel, to this gift of a holiday in the snow, I won't risk anything but the truth. To myself, to her.

I've been a liar. A cheat. An asshole, a bastard, a fucking fool.

I won't do that again.

We go snowshoeing until Hazel's nose is pink and her eyes

are bright, then we head back inside and dress for dinner. She wears a touchable white sweater shot through with silver sparkles that sways low across the tops of her breasts, showing the edge of a snug black tank top. It's distractingly festive.

On the way to the dining room, I tell Hazel to head in ahead of me, because I need to hit the little boys' room. But instead I dodge back to the lobby, to the gift shop we've looked in a few times, and buy her a necklace.

The seventh date is a perfectly acceptable point to start gifting jewellery.

She'd talked about buying a stone loon sculpture for her desk, so I choose a necklace from the same artist. A loon in flight, polished smooth, hanging on a thin gold chain.

"Can you wrap that for me?"

"Oui, monsieur, of course." The clerk smiles. "A last-minute Christmas gift?"

"Yes. For my girlfriend." I grin. That sounds good. "Do you have any gift tags?"

She hands one over, then turns away to wrap the small, square box.

I look at the blank tag. What would capture this moment where we're at, between old desire and new discoveries?

After some thought, I scrawl a quick message, then attach it to the ribbon.

When I arrive in the dining room, Hazel has ordered us a bottle of wine. She stops mid-pour when I set the present in front of her. Her eyes linger there for a moment before she lifts her gaze to my face. "What is this?"

"A little something to mark what is the best Christmas of my life," I say gruffly.

"Aww, Sam." She makes a scrunchy face, her eyes bright again, and this time not from the cold. "I have something for you, too. Do you want to order for us, and I'll dash up and get it? Or do you want to save this for later and we can open them both in our room?"

I look at the smooth curve of her neck, the bare space above her tank top. The necklace would look perfect with her sweater. "You can open it now."

She shakes her head. "Then I'm getting yours, too, because it's only fair. Be right back." She stands, then stops beside me. "Thank you," she whispers, leaning in to brush her mouth against mine.

Warmth floods my chest.

It barely takes her any time at all to return, a small paper-wrapped package in her hand. Not Christmas paper, I realize. She's wrapped it roughly in newspaper from our room.

"I didn't know you were going to give me something, so I was just going to shove this at you tomorrow." She sits down across from me and holds it out. "Merry Christmas, Sam."

I take it, and from the weight and feel of it, I know it's a book.

My pulse jacks back up as I peel back the newsprint.

It's hers, I know it is, and when the cover is revealed, a black and white photo of a couple in an embrace, I'm speechless. *Entwined* is the title.

She's trusted me with this, and I know the value of that.

I trace the name on the cover. Aibhlin Moon. "So that's your pen name."

She nods. "Yep."

"This is amazing." I turn it over and read her biography on the back.

Aibhlin Moon lives by herself in a small house in a small town, where she scribbles down big ideas.

"How many books do you have out?"

"A bunch."

"I'm buying them all. I want them signed."

"I'll give them to you."

I shake my head. "I'm ordering them as soon as I get home. I've got a bookstore connection."

"Sam…" She trails off, then nods. "Okay. Cool. I'll happily sign them for you."

"Naked."

Her cheeks turn pink and she looks around the dining room. "Yes," she whispers when she looks back. "Naked."

"Good. Now, your turn."

She picks up the box and looks at the card first. I like the way she bites her lip as she reads what I wrote.

For Hazel, full of grace and perfect in every way.
Love, Sam

I'd gone back and forth on whether to slide that on the end, but it's a card. It's allowed.

She carefully peels off the wrapping and opens the box.

"Oh, it's…wow." She drags in a breath, then looks up at me. "Nice. So nice, Sam, you didn't have to."

"I wanted to. I wanted you to have something to remember this trip by, and you seemed to like the loons."

She stands up again, coming around to my side of the table. "Help me put it on?"

I stand, too, not caring that people are glancing our way. I take the chain from her and set it around her neck, fastening the clasp first, then dropping a soft kiss to the bare skin just above it.

THE REST of the evening slowly unfurls like a holiday movie montage. Mulled cider, live music by the fireplace in the lobby, a long, sweet kiss under mistletoe we find by the elevator.

And then the montage fades to black as we tumble into bed, those hotter moments just for us.

On Christmas Day, we wake up slowly. I want to fuck her, hold her, make love to her, but there will be time for that soon enough. When we get to her place, or maybe mine.

I don't care where we go next as long as we're still together a while longer.

So when we're both fully awake, and she crawls on top of me, I kiss her. Long and slow, full of promise.

Then we shower, pack, and head to the dining room for breakfast before we check out. And we're spoiled by the wait staff. Fancy coffee, sparkling mimosas, and heaping plates loaded down with a proper French Canadian breakfast. Crepes, sausages, maple baked beans, thick slices of roast ham and the best hollandaise sauce poured over the most perfect poached eggs I've ever had.

Hazel's quietly laughing at me as I devour my food.

"What?"

"You're like a kid in a candy shop this morning."

"It's a good breakfast."

"It's the same breakfast we had yesterday." She smiles softly.

I know. But it's our last one, and this has been…something. Something amazing, something special, something I don't want to forget. "It's different this morning."

She nods, her gaze lingering on my face. "Yeah."

Everything is different now.

And it's too soon to talk about that. So much has happened, so much water under the bridge, but *we* are still new.

11

HAZEL

Sam drives me all the way home to Stratford and stays in my bed for two more days before finally leaving to get back to the real world and his job.

We don't talk about this burgeoning relationship, and what comes next.

We talk about books and food and movies. We spend a good amount of time not talking at all, just cuddling and fucking and reading.

"Will you come to the city for New Year's Eve?" he asks me when we're naked, putting me at a terrible disadvantage.

I beam and tell him of course. "But I have to do some work first."

"I understand."

"How will we ring in the new year?"

"Alex hosts a party."

"Sounds fun."

Sam makes a face.

"Ah. Will your brother be there?"

"Yeah." He growls and pulls me on top of him. "But so will a lot of other people. Enough of that."

Fucking, cuddling, and reading together.

It's bliss.

And when he leaves, I open my computer and start writing.

12

SAM

SHE SHOWS up on my doorstep four days later, a day before I expect her for New Year's Eve. "Hi," she says when I open the door. "Is it okay that I'm here?"

I sweep her into my arms. "Get your ass inside. I've missed you."

She laughs and crawls up my body, her mouth hot and eager. "I hope I didn't interrupt any plans? You said you were making dinner when I texted you..."

"Trying to, anyway."

She gives me a shy look. "Can I help?"

My chest squeezes. "Yes. Fuck, yes. Please." I lead her into the apartment. "It's my resolution for next year. I'm starting early. I want to actually use my kitchen and be a human."

"Less takeout, more..." She stops as she takes in the chaos in my kitchen. "How many different pans do you have going?"

"I thought I'd cook ahead for your visit. That's, uh,

spaghetti sauce, and those are sautéed vegetables. I've also got chicken breasts in the oven and—" I cut myself off. "All of the pans, apparently."

It's overboard, I know it is, but we have a lot of time to make up for.

"Well…" She moves around the island, looking at the mess. "Can I start with these mushrooms? What are they for?"

"I was going to stuff them. An appetizer. Or dinner while I texted with you later tonight, if they didn't turn out well enough to save for tomorrow."

She laughs and picks up a paring knife. "Got it."

Since I was mostly done the other dishes, I turn to clean-up duty while she preps the mushrooms, then switches knives and begins mincing garlic for the stuffing.

I stop tidying and give in to my urge to just watch her hands flash over the cutting board. Chop, chop, gather, chop, chop, drag. She lifts her head to look at me. "Can you grate some salt on this?"

Fuck, how happy does it make me to cook with her? I add the salt to her board, then stick right next to her as she does a final pass on the garlic.

It's perfectly minced.

"Good job," I murmur, kissing her soundly.

I like the way she blushes when I pull away. "I don't cook a lot. But when I do, I like to do it well."

"It's sexy. I got half-hard watching your hands, your arms. Watching you work."

"Get out of here."

I move behind her, bracketing her against the island. "Feel how worked up I am, imagining those clever fingers wrapped around my cock instead of the knife. And you'd have that same adorable frown of concentration as you stroke me faster and faster, trying to make me come."

She shivers. "Ah, I see what you're trying to do, Mr. Distraction."

I kiss her neck. "Not at all. Just being honest."

She smiles. "I like it. I want to hear more after dinner."

I take the hint and move away. "What else should we talk about?"

Her head tilts to the side.

I like that I can read her like a book. "Ask me anything, Hazel. I told you that when you came here the first time, and I meant it. We've got ten minutes before the chicken is done."

"I…" She rolls her lips together. "It's…"

I get a bottle of wine and two glasses out. She watches me, but she doesn't say anything else.

Holding my arms out, I gesture for her. "Come here."

She folds in against me.

"Why did you show up a day early?"

A soft sigh flutters against my shirt. "I was feeling a bit anxious. I wanted to see you. It's hard to remember that this is real when you're elsewhere. Does that make any sense in a non-creepy way?"

"Sure. You don't know if I'm a long term safe bet. I get that. You don't need to trust that I've changed. I'll show you. All I want is a chance to keep showing you who I am, and how I feel about you. And you know, make you feel good."

She blushes. "I like all of that."

"Especially the last part?"

"Yes."

"How do you want me to make you feel good tonight?"

She gives me a searching look.

I touch my finger to her chin and lift her face so I can lean in and kiss her. Soft, at first, then harder, our tongues sliding and teasing. Arousing. "I'll do anything you want."

"Hold me down in bed," she whispers. "Be big on top of me."

"Deal." I suck in a rough breath. "Should I turn off the stove?"

She shakes her head, but kisses me again before answering. "Let's eat. Let's talk. We'll have all night in bed after that."

I pour the wine and she puts the mushrooms in the oven, then I pull her back into my arms.

"What else do you want to know?"

"Anything. Everything. I don't even know where to start."

"Do you want to know about the gambling?" She hasn't asked. Maybe she never would, so I'm putting it on the table.

She pulls back and gives me a warm, steady look. "Yes. If you want to share."

I nod slowly. "Sure." I squeeze her hip, then step back, needing a bit of space. "It started in high school. It filled a hole. No, a lot of holes, not just one. My life was pretty empty. I didn't have a girlfriend until I went to university, and God knows why Regan stayed with me."

Something flashes across Hazel's face, and she glances away.

Nervous guilt lances through me, but it doesn't belong. "What is it?"

"I didn't understand why she stayed with you either," she mutters. Then she looks back at me, from beneath her lashes, dark and sooty. A confessional kind of look. "I never understood her attraction to you."

Her lips twist, and the nervous feeling flutters away. Turns filthy instead.

"Never?"

She makes a rueful face. "Nope."

"Wow."

"But…" She trails off. Winks. "But deep down, I knew. Because I wanted that guy, too. Broken, off-limits Sam. Dangerously attractive to us all."

Fuck. "That's not who I am now."

"I know." She rubs my arm, and I cover her hand with mine. "I don't *want* that guy. I just—now—can admit that I was drawn to him against my better judgement. And I'm drawn to *you* with all of my heart."

"I'm glad." I stroke her cheek. "Can I confess something that doesn't put me in the best of lights?"

"Always."

"I never really trusted that relationship. Or any other, for a long time. There are a lot of labels I've learned since then to explain what I'd gotten wrapped up in. Grandiosity is the best one, because it captures the worst of it. The vanity. The rush of success. Victory. But it's a lie, because nothing ever stuck. No high was big enough. And the crashes got worse, so the next bet had to be bigger. It was…intense."

"I'm sorry," she says softly, and I shake my head.

"No. Thank you, but no. I did it to myself. And then I got into the more complicated shit. Secrets and lies, trading on information I learned in card games. I could see the crash coming, and I didn't care." I exhaled hard.

She moves in front of me and wraps her arms around my waist.

A hug. No words, no apologies that aren't hers to give, or mine to ever ask for. Just a warm, sweet embrace.

I kiss her temple and let her give me that.

I WAKE up in the middle of the night and realize Hazel's beside me, wide awake. I mumble her name as I reach for her. "What's wrong?"

"Nothing." Her voice is light, and when she turns her head in my direction, I can make out the gentle curve of a smile. "Sometimes I can't sleep, that's all. I was thinking."

"About what?"

"Stories." She curls into my side. "But you should go back to sleep."

"I can't do that now. I want to know about the story."

"It's filthy."

"More poems inspired by Sam Preston?"

She laughs and shifts closer. "We should bottle and sell your ego. It's quite the thing."

I brush my lips against her neck. "Not lately."

"Could have fooled me."

"I don't want to fool you about anything," I whisper. She twists in my arms. I kiss her, hard, and she makes a sound that I like, so I do it again.

Then I tumble her beneath me, wedge myself between her legs. She's slick, welcoming, but I don't rush. My cock throbs to be inside her, to feel her tight warmth. *I* throb to get lost in this moment.

But she's the one who couldn't sleep. "What do you want?"

"You." She stretches her arms up and around me. "Inside me."

"I was thinking the same thing." I notch my cock at her entrance, and she squirms. "Yes?"

She nods.

So I press the crown inside her, just the tip, and my balls pull tight. She feels so good, impossibly soft and wet, and my cock strains at the restraint.

The way Hazel whimpers, she's feeling some way about being denied, too.

I brace my arm beside her head, caging her in as I swivel my hips. Just the tip, throbbing thick and hard against her body. Inside her body, but just barely.

When she bucks her hips, I pull back, my dick waving free before slapping down on her clit. She reaches for me, and I grab her hand.

"Wait for it," I growl.

Her eyes go wide. Then she grins and slowly shakes her head. "Make me," she whispers. "If you want to torture me."

I pin her arm her her head, stretching her out. I can hold

both of her arms down with one hand and tease every inch of her body with the other if she's going to be like that. "You don't think I want to be buried inside you already?"

"I know you do." Her breath catches.

"This is torture for us both. But it feels good, too. Doesn't it?"

"Yes."

I squeeze her wrists. "Good. Now…" I tease the entrance to her pussy again. "What was your story idea?"

She gasps, then groans my name.

"You don't need to tell me," I whisper, taking my cock away from where it desperately wants to be.

"This isn't fair."

"I could go back to sleep." I feign closing my eyes and dropping my head next to hers.

She howls and bucks her hips, trying to connect our bodies.

I surge against her, grinding and bucking and not giving her what we both want.

"It was about rope," she whispers.

"The castle idea?"

She hesitates. "No. Yes, but not. Something different."

I kiss her hard on the mouth. "Thank you for sharing." I like the way she shivers as I fit us together and sink into her, filling her up with my cock—finally. "Thank you for telling me."

"It's—ah!" She rolls her head back. And whatever she was going to say is lost as I lick the sweet expanse her neck, as I gather her in my arms and move us together, rough at first, then frantically. It's a hard, fast fuck that gets us both to a gasping conclusion.

And then sleep pulls me under again, this time with Hazel pinned against my side.

13

HAZEL

SAM'S ROOM is bright when I wake up, and a glance at the bedside clock tells me it's almost noon. With a squawk, I jump out of bed and pull on clothes.

I find him in the living room, sprawled out on the couch. He's reading.

And when I realize *what* he's reading, I skid to a halt.

He looks up, slowly, and gives me a grin. It's a knowing, filthy grin, and from the roughly even divide of pages read and pages still-to-be-read, he's at the midpoint of my book. There's usually sex thereabouts, and that's fine, I'm proud of my work, but it's still *weird*. "Good morning," he murmurs.

"Barely," I whisper, my gaze jerking back to his hands, holding my book open. "I didn't mean to sleep in."

"You needed it." He closes the book and sets it down on the coffee table. To my delight and horror, a strange combination of feelings, I realize the copy of *Entwined* that I gave him is not the only book of mine he owns. There's a stack of them. A book of poetry, and a couple of novels.

"Sam?"

He gives me an innocent look. "Yes?"

"Did you..." I gesture at the books, because he clearly did. "Buy my books?"

"I told you, I'm considering becoming a patron of the arts."

"This feels more like research than an investment."

"Oh, it's an investment, all right." He stands up. "Are you hungry?"

Is that the end of that conversation? But my stomach growls. "Yes."

"Do you want to cook together, or go out?"

I want him to explain why he's reading my books. *An investment.* "You know I am not my books, right?"

"Right." He crosses to me, brushes his lips against mine, then turns me around and points me to the kitchen. "Cook together it is. Shall we make pancakes?"

"There are pancakes in that book!"

"I noticed." I can feel his silent laughter against my back as he wraps his arms around me. "Are you okay?"

"No."

The way he shakes, his body big and hard and also soft, somehow, understanding, tells me he gets the nuances I've poured into that single syllable. "Would pancakes make you feel better?"

I smile to myself, glad he can't see my face. "Yes."

"My investment is paying off already." He wraps one arm tight around my waist, holding me in place, and uses his other hand to lift my hair out of the way so he can kiss the back of my neck.

Pancakes. That was the first "secret to Hazel" he took from reading my books. Not the dirty talk, or the spanking—I try to remember all the sex scenes I wrote in that book, but I definitely remember a heavy emphasis on the spanking.

Not for the first time, I picture Sam putting me over his lap.

I squirm against him as he kisses my neck. "That's my girl," he murmurs. "She likes pancakes, and neck kisses, and surprises."

"Surprises?" My voice catches.

"Mm-hmm. Like showing up here a day early. You couldn't help yourself, and we both liked that surprise. And discovering me reading your books. That was a surprise, and you liked it."

"I think I clearly displayed my reaction."

"I saw delighted surprise."

"Pretty sure it was more of a disquieted uncertainty."

He laughs out loud. "Disquieted uncertainty?" Spinning me around, he grabs me by the hips and hoists me into the air. "Hold on tight, funny girl."

I squeal and wrap my arms around him as he carries me into the kitchen and deposits me on the counter.

Then he braces his hands on either side of me and leans in, resting his forehead against mine. "Hazel," he whispers, his eyes dancing. "I have a confession to make."

"You don't know how to make pancakes?"

"I'm confident I can figure it out." He kisses me. "But I'm

going to need to you to close your eyes for a minute while I Google it."

I giggle and squeeze my eyelids shut. "Deal." But he doesn't move. "Are you staring at me?"

"Guilty."

"Sam..."

He kisses me softly, his lips lingering against mine. I keep my eyes closed the whole time. Ignore my pounding heart, my complicated feelings. I ignore everything except the way his mouth feels, the taste of his skin, the slide of his tongue. Simple, pure, good.

"I have ten years of kissing to make up for," he finally says roughly. "And I like to look at you. Is that okay?"

I nod.

And I keep my eyes squeezed shut.

It's more than okay.

So why did I trip over my own feet when I saw him reading my book, a copy I gave him myself?

ONE OF SAM'S clients has a panicky meltdown about a stock price changing that afternoon, so he goes out for a few hours.

I do a bit of work, then curl up on his couch and pick up the book of poetry. My book, in Sam's condo. My book, with the spine cracked, and despite his cocky teasing, it's not the poem about himself that the book falls open to.

It's a poem about friendship, and absence.

Growling at my past self for being a better person than my present self, I grab my phone and send Regan a quick text.

Hazel: Hey stranger! Hope you guys had a good Christmas.
Regan: Were your ears burning? I was just talking about you.

I hit the call button, and she answers right away. There's noise in the background, laughing and talking.

"Is this a bad time?"

"Not at all. Hang on, let me just escape..." She sighs a moment later. "That's better. My sister's family is here."

"Fun." I pick at the blanket I've wrapped myself in. "Hey, so...weird that you were just talking about me. I was just thinking about you."

"Aww. The universe works in mysterious ways. Did you guess my news?"

"Nope." I take a deep breath, willing my chest to relax. "Tell me."

"I'm pregnant again."

"Oh, wow." I laugh, and then shake my head—at myself—glad she can't see me. "That's exciting."

"I'm almost five months along, but we held off on telling people this time..." She trailed off.

I remember her last pregnancy announcement being followed by sad news. "I understand," I say softly. "I'm thrilled for you both."

"Thanks. So, why were you thinking of me?"

I glance at the poem in my lap. "Something weird happened just before Christmas. I ran into Sam on the train. Your Sam."

Those two words don't feel right at all, not together, and *whoa*, I wasn't expecting to feel quite like this, like maybe I've done something wrong, but also that it doesn't feel wrong, and wishing history had gone a different way.

"Sam Preston?" She whistles. "Wow. How is he?"

Complicated. Beautiful. "I'm actually in his apartment right now. He's…good."

She doesn't reply right away.

This was a mistake.

I'm not looking for permission.

"Are you seeing each other?" she finally asks.

I can't read her tone over the phone. "Yes."

"Ah."

"Reg—"

"I'm happy for you," she says in a rush. "That came across wrong. But I'm surprised, that's all."

"That makes two of us." Three of us, probably, but I don't want to assume. And even if I am right, I want to keep that part of Sam to myself.

"He wrote to me last year. Do you know…?"

"I think so. He told me about his legal troubles."

She exhales. "Good." Another pause. "He must have changed a lot in ten years, for you to give him a chance."

"He spent the morning reading my books."

"Really?"

I frown. "Yes."

"He has changed. Reading is hard for him."

Now I'm the one who's shocked. "Really? I don't remember that. I saw him in the library all the time." Which doesn't mean anything, now that I say it out loud.

"Don't tell him I said anything," she says gently. "But… yeah. It was a big deal for him growing up. He never told me about it, but there were clues along the way. Dismissive things his family would say."

"Did you ever meet them?"

She made a thinking sound. "His brother was on campus. There was a girlfriend…I liked her a lot. Grace."

"They got married," I added.

"Huh." It was a loaded reaction.

"What about his parents?"

"Only in passing. His father gave a presentation at the business school, and then took Sam and Luke out for dinner. Sam showed up at my place drunk afterwards. It was…not good."

I've pried enough. If I want to know more about Sam's family, I should ask Sam himself. "He really has changed," I tell my friend. "And he asked about you."

"Tell him I'm sorry I never replied to his letter. I didn't know how to take it."

"I will." I smile. "Hey, send me a picture of the baby bump, okay?"

"Deal. Merry Christmas."

14

SAM

HAZEL IS fresh out of the shower when I return, her hair damp. She's wearing skimpy slips of silk, a barely there bra and tiny panties, standing in the middle of my bedroom.

It looks like a bomb has gone off, and I swear she didn't bring this many clothes with her.

"Can I help you choose an outfit?" I ask from the doorway.

She jumps in the air. "Oh!"

"Did you not hear me come in?"

"I was lost in thought." She gestured to the clothes. "But yes, please help. What are you wearing tonight?"

"I usually wear a suit, but I can dress down if you want. There will be people in jeans." I glance at her options, which are all lovely. "I would rather coordinate with you than vice versa."

She picks up a black dress and pulls it over her head, hiding her silky undergarments, but I know they're there.

They will tease me all night.

"Maybe this, with tall boots? If I can wear the boots inside his house? Is that—"

I cross to her and kiss her to slow her down. "That's fine. This crowd doesn't take off their shoes."

She wrinkles her nose against mine. "Messy."

"Alex can afford a cleaner to polish his floors again."

"Well la di da, Mr. Rock—" She giggles as I cut her off again with my mouth. Then she sighs as I hike the dress up enough to palm her ass and tug her whole body hard against mine. "I need to do my hair and make up."

"I like the panties."

"Do you?"

"I'll like them even more about your ankles when we get back from the party." I stroke my fingers between her legs. "Or during the party, if you're game."

She sighs happily. "How private are the corners of his house?"

"Very."

THE LIGHTS ARE BLAZING on every floor of Alex's gothic mansion just off Dupont. I open the door without knocking and usher Hazel inside.

She winks at me as she brushes past. "Very private corners, you say?"

I grin. "Just you wait."

A staircase inside the foyer winds upstairs, and it's littered with people. Some I recognize, most I don't. Alex has an eclectic mix of friends from the business and literary worlds, as well as people he's picked up along the way in his various hobbies. Hockey, music.

The party will spill throughout the house, but we don't go upstairs first. I lead her past Alex's office, a dark, gloomy library that might serve as the dark corner we want later in the evening, and into the open great room beyond. He took out a few walls to make a free flowing space, part dining room, part kitchen, all party space.

Conversations compete to rise above the fray, words popping here and there. Investment. Release date. Publicist. Hazel's eyes light up, and I remember what she told me about story ideas. She sees people, hears snippets, and the inspiration comes from a collision of individual pieces.

Alex is holding court at one end of the dining table, and when he sees us, he waves us over.

"Hazel," he says, greeting my date warmly. "You survived the trip?"

"We had fun," she says. "Thank you for helping us out."

"Anything for a fellow writer."

"I'm just chopped liver, I guess?" I hold out my hand and we shake.

Alex grins. "Did you get her pen name out of her?"

"I did."

"And it is…?"

I glance at Hazel, who presses her lips together. Mums the word.

"A secret," I say without pause. Hazel leans into me. Damn straight.

"Sorry, Alex," she says. "But I like the air of mystery."

He throws his head back and laughs. "I understand completely. Let me introduce you to a couple of people..."

After making the rounds, we dig into the food he's had catered. The next two hours spin by, Hazel never far from my side. I like the way she touches me unconsciously, with little leans and one-arm hugs.

I've never brought a date to a party like this, and it makes the whole evening more fun. The best part is the secret glances. Hazel has this way of biting her bottom lip that looks like she's concentrating deeply on what someone is saying, but it's really keeping her from laughing.

I want to bite that lip myself.

I want to swallow her laughter and share the inside joke.

As we return to the buffet for a third round of nibbles, I catch the same look on her face—but nobody is around us. I glance left and right, then lower my voice to a conspiratorial note. "What is it?"

"Maybe nothing," she murmurs. "But I recognize someone here, and it's... Alex has a weird mix of friends."

"Yeah. Who is it?"

"That guy behind you—don't look too fast—at six o'clock, the one with the beard. I recognize him."

Just as I'm about to casually glance around, I hear my name. Which is a great excuse to turn quickly, check out the big bearded dude Hazel is talking about, then wave to my brother and Grace who have just arrived.

My brother waves, but heads straight to the kitchen for a drink.

Grace beelines for me—or rather, Hazel, who is the only person in the room she has eyes for.

I guess we're not going to talk about how Hazel knows the bearded guy.

A throb of…not jealousy, but maybe curiosity…tugs at my gut. Like she was going to share something weird, and I want that. I want all of her weird secrets to be my weird secrets, too.

Right now is not that moment, though. I take a swallow of wine, a palate cleanser, before making introductions.

"Hazel, this is my sister-in-law Grace."

"I've heard so much about you," Hazel says warmly, holding out her hand.

Grace takes it with both of hers and shakes. "And I have not heard nearly enough about you. Sam is keeping you all to himself, and I object."

"Do you, now?" I ask dryly. Then I wrap my arm around my girlfriend.

"You don't need to protect her from me," Grace protests. "Hazel, can I steal you away?"

Hazel glances at me, her eyes twinkling. "Are you okay if Grace grills me?"

"Do I get a choice?"

She leans in and kisses me. "I'll be back to finish our conversation soon."

15

HAZEL

I DON'T KNOW what I was expecting of Sam's sister-in-law, who filled his loft with erotic art, and also calls him in the middle of the night in a panic, but it wasn't this chaotic, bubbly ping-pong ball of a person. She's little, barely over five feet, and as polished as Sam is, she's his complete opposite.

When he said some people would be in jeans, he clearly meant Grace.

I think she has paint under her fingernails, too.

Her jeans look expensive, of course, as does her hair cut. But her face is bare, and the t-shirt she is wearing under a silk blazer reads *Dogs Adored, Humans Tolerated.*

Her priorities cannot be faulted.

She drags me upstairs, dodging people sitting on the stairs, and pulls me into a more casual living room than the open space downstairs. There's a couple making out in the corner, but Grace doesn't pay them any attention. She sits in an armchair and pats the couch beside her. "Come. Sit. Tell me everything."

"About what?"

"About you. All I know is that Sam bumped into you on the train, and you went to school together. Which means we technically went to school together, too, but I was a few years ahead of you."

"It's a small world." I'm grinning, because despite my preconceived ideas of who she is, I like her—a lot. But I don't know how much I want to tell her. I don't know how much I want to tell anyone, about anything, ever. I'm a single child and an introvert. My life does not need to be a shared experience with the world.

"What do you do?"

"I'm a writer."

"Do you know Alex, then?"

"We've just met once. Well, twice, I suppose now."

"So you don't move in his circles?"

My lips twitch. "No."

"What do you write?"

"Erotica. Under a secret pen name."

She gasps and claps her hands. "I make erotic art!"

"I know. Your pieces in Sam's apartment are beautiful."

"They aren't all my work, but I sourced them for him. Only because he didn't care, and I didn't want his space to be completely soulless, you know?"

There's something in how she says it, an urgency, a protective instinct, that softens my guard. "You wanted to make it nice for him."

"He deserves that."

I nod. "He's grateful, too."

Her highlighted blonde waves bob as she agrees. "He's always so good about making that clear. He's come a long way."

The second time today I've talked about that. "I know. I really like him," I assured her. "A lot."

"Good. He's sensitive, you know."

"I do." I glance around. The making-out couple are talking now, quiet giggles. "So you know Alex through Luke?"

"They went to business school together."

"Ah."

She laughs. "That's a loaded *ah*."

"Oh, I'm sorry, did you got to business school, too?"

"Good lord, no. I was an art major. And then I let the business people around me steer me in the wrong direction for a while—I worked in galleries—but I'm back in the muck now, and loving it."

"Same for me, sort of." When she raises her eyebrows, eager for more, I soften all the way. "I had middle-class parents very concerned I wouldn't be able to afford a mortgage if I wrote full time, so I juggled writing a and a day job for far too long."

Her eyes light up. "So you're in the muck now, too?"

"I guess so."

"That's even better." She taps her lower lip with her index finger. "Can I ask if I might have read your work?"

"Depends how much you've read."

"So I can ask, but you won't answer?"

I laugh. "Tell me a few authors you've read, and I'll tell you if you're in the right direction."

"Just how secret is your writing?" She looks delighted at the prospect.

"It's...those middle-class parents I mentioned. They don't know what I write. I like it that way. I like that I don't have to ever ask myself, what would Mom think? Because Mom is never going to know. I want to think I'm not susceptible to that dampening filter, but I would be. So...it's pretty secret."

"Then I won't even guess," she says resolutely. "But if I ever figure it out, your secret is safe with me."

"Thank you." I wish I could tell her that her secret is safe with me, too, but I don't even know what it is other than her husband is clearly a jackass.

"I'm so glad for Sam that he's found you again. He needs a bit of that."

The subject of our conversation strolls in just in time to hear that. He's two glasses of wine, and he hands one to me. The other he keeps firmly for himself as he gives his sister-in-law a reproachful look. "Hey, now."

Grace waves him off. "I mean it with love."

"And that love is felt right here." He taps himself on the chest and mimes being wounded. "Your husband is picking a fight about hockey."

She makes a face. "All right. I'll go and rescue...who is he arguing with?"

"A forward for the Maple Leafs."

I laugh, I can't help it.

"Sorry," I whisper when they both look at me.

Grace sighs. "No, it's funny. I'll see you later?"

"Yep." I catch her hand and squeeze. "Thanks for the talk. It was nice getting to know each other a bit."

"We'll do it again."

"Can I give you a tour of the rest of the place while we have a bit of privacy?" Sam asks as he leads me back to the landing. Another staircase goes to the third floor, and it's dark up there.

This doesn't stop him from urging me up there.

"Are we finding a private corner to fool around in? That seems to be a theme tonight, although the couple I saw didn't bother to find a corner."

He laughs under his breath. "I'm not into being watched, no worries."

As soon as I step into the dark shadows on the top floor, Sam wraps his arms around me and pulls me snug against his body. "We have an unfinished conversation."

"Do we?" I twist and kiss his neck.

"You were going to tell me something about that man downstairs."

"Oh, him."

Sam tugs my hair, his grip loose but firm. "Do you know him?"

"I know of him."

"And who is he?"

"I'm not sure if I should say. It occurred to me when I was

talking to Grace that some people are very private."

"Is he one of them?"

"I dunno." I swallow a strange, trembling feeling. "I was talking about me."

"I like how private you are," he murmurs. "Mysterious. A puzzle for me to solve."

"I like to be private with you, too," I whisper. I drop to my knees and fumble for his belt.

He gathers my hair in his hands again. I can't see him, but I can feel him. The strain of his thighs, the throb of his cock.

And I can hear him, bossy utterances whispered for my ears only. "Swallow me. Go back downstairs with a full belly."

Heat flames through me, bright licks of desire. I wrap my fingers around his length, heavy and silky smooth, and part my lips. I'm eager to taste him, to feel that weight on my tongue. He fills my mouth and then some, but I can take it.

I'll take everything he gives me.

16

SAM

I FUCK her mouth quietly at the top of the stairs. We should go to a room, any room, and close the door. Find a wall I can plow her against, but it's too late.

As soon as Hazel dropped to her knees, I was gone.

Her mouth feels fantastic, hot and wet, and as I mutter what I want to do—come in her mouth, fill her up, make her swallow every last drop—I get there.

Fast.

Furious.

The corners of my vision blurs, the darkness spinning into a murky kaleidoscope as her mouth gets sloppy, taking even more of me than before.

She groans, a desperate, gagging sound that fucking makes me feel like a filthy monster, and I lose it. Pumping my hips one last time, rubbing that spot on the bottom of my cock head against her tongue—fuck, yes—my orgasm explodes, spurting against the back of her throat.

With a happy sound, she swallows, then tightens her lips around my cock—so fucking sensitive, Jesus—and cleans me up.

Hot. Fucking. Damn.

I ease out of her mouth and reach for the wall, dragging new breath into my chest.

From the floor, Hazel giggles softly.

I reach for her blindly and pull her up, then press her against the wall.

From downstairs, we can hear the faint countdown to midnight. *Ten, nine…* I ease my fingers into her pussy and find her clit with my thumb.

"Your turn," I growl as I kiss her sweet, abused mouth. I suck on her talented tongue and bite her precious lips.

As the clock strikes midnight and everyone bursts into song, I grab Hazel and stumble into the nearest room, a spare bedroom, and shove the door shut behind me. She lands on the bed, on her back, and all I can make out are pale thighs surrounded by a black dress and black boots.

"I want these over my shoulders," I mutter as I fall on her.

My mouth finds her silky panties first, then my fingers. I tug them aside and sink into the sticky sweet mess of her pussy. I'm going to wear the scent of her on me for the rest of the night, and I don't fucking care.

She tastes like heaven. Like a special kind of salvation I didn't know I still had the capacity to hope for.

My Hazel.

Mine.

※

It's nearly three in the morning when we get in the car to go back to my place. Hazel is half asleep against me.

But when we arrive home, she doesn't let me tuck her straight into bed.

She stops me as I'm peeling off her boots. "I wanted to tell you…I told Regan about us today. Earlier."

I sit back on my heels. "How'd that go?"

"She says she got your letter, and she's sorry she didn't reply."

"Ah." I shrug. "Nothing to be sorry for."

She nods. "I know."

I stand up and strip out of my clothes. She waited until the end of the night to tell me about the conversation for a reason. "Was there something else?"

Hazel scoots back and climbs under the blanket, waits for me to join her before answering. "She said she didn't want me to get hurt."

"I'm not going to hurt you," I say levelly. It doesn't offend me, because I know my own truth. "Ever."

"I believe you," she says softly, tracing her fingertips featherlight along my jaw. "I might be the one to hurt you."

Maybe our New Year's Resolution could be to not hurt each other. But I don't say that out loud.

17

HAZEL

Winter storms and train schedules seem determined to conspire to ruin my best-laid plans again. Sam is coming to Stratford for the weekend, but his train out of Toronto is delayed.

Story of our relationship—winter in southwestern Ontario being what it is.

Our long distance relationship isn't as long distance as some others, but it's still been annoying to manage at times, especially as January zoomed into February and work got insane for both of us. I've spent the last month on deadline and Sam has had a rough time with his brother Luke, too, not that he talks about it much.

When he texts today to say he's finally on the way, almost two hours late, I burst into tears of relief.

There is no good explanation for why I feel so desperate at losing a few hours out of our weekend. We see each other more than I've ever spent with any previous boyfriend.

But there's an anxiety deep inside me that won't go away. Like we need more time together, more conversations, more connection, before taking the final leap and admitting…all the things one might be reluctant to admit about a guy who one is head-over-something for, but super nervous about saying what that something is because of historical dysfunction.

His.

Mine.

Ours.

Instead of dwelling on feelings that are best left unnamed, I wipe my happy-sad eyes and I throw myself into a hot shower to erase the evidence that I'm a giant suck. Also to get myself squeaky clean for the terrible things Sam's going to spend the afternoon doing to me.

After my shower, I try to get a bit more work done, but I finally give up on that and do all the pre-boyfriend-visit things like change my sheets, put beer in the fridge, and re-stock the condom bowl beside the bed—and the mini one in the bathroom, for eventual shower sex.

Then I dress in sexy lingerie, and because it's winter in southwestern Ontario, I cover that up with two layers of unsexy warmth. I'm only a ten-minute walk to the train station, but ten minutes in the freezing cold is still too much.

And still Sam is worth it.

Sam, who a decade earlier had been the worst boyfriend ever to my best friend. Sam, who made the worst decisions possible for a very long time.

Sam.

I never would have imagined.

And there's that feeling again, the scary I-don't-want-to-say-it feeling.

Because he's also the first boyfriend I've ever had who straight-up owns all of his feelings, good and bad. Who catches himself in any kind of white lie or "harmless fib", because he knows they aren't harmless.

He's also the first guy I've ever dated who has been up—or down—for literally anything I want to do in the bedroom. Or what I want *him* to do to *me*. Like pretend I'm too scared to sleep alone when he rescues me in a dark, forbidden forest.

Think of the filthy, happy sex, Hazel.

Oh, I am.

This week I had a chimney sweep come and service my rarely used fireplace. Yesterday I bought two bags of firewood so Sam can role-play my woodcutter fantasy this weekend.

"I wrote you another story..." It has become my calling card. They aren't all for *him*, technically. But he enjoys every single word.

And I enjoy the reactions I get.

That happy thought keeps me warm all the way to the train station. I get there with a few minutes to spare.

They drag by like hours.

The hot, prickly, confusing tears threaten again when the train finally pulls in, but the sheer joy at seeing him stride through the doors—finally—wins out.

I throw myself into his arms as he drops his bag beside us.

"I'm sorry I'm late," he murmurs against my mouth.

I squeeze him tight. It doesn't matter. He's here now. "I missed you."

Three little words. Not the really big, truly scary ones, but they're raw and honest, and that's scary enough. He goes still around me, then his arms squeeze back. Big, strong, secure. But also shaking, just a little.

"Sam?"

He kisses me again, his lips soft. "I miss you, too. All the time. This is hard."

We're in the middle of the train station. This isn't the place, but whatever. We weren't supposed to ever talk again. He was supposed to be all wrong for me.

Maybe nothing is supposed to go the way we think.

"I cried when you messaged that your train was going to be late," I confess. "It feels like we're living in a few hours here and there, and losing any of them is upsetting. More than it should be, to be honest."

There it is again. Should.

I breathe in deeply and tangle my fingers in his hair. "I want more—"

"I love you."

"—time," I whisper, because I was mid thought and his rough words don't register at first. "No pressure."

Wait. What?

His eyes are impossibly bright. He's smiling now, carefully. *I love you.*

We stand there, entwined in the middle of Stratford's wee train station. Thank God I live in a town full of overwrought drama types, because this is nothing here, but somewhere else it might be a real scene.

He loves me?

"No pressure," he says gruffly.

"That was my line," I squeak.

"It was a good one."

"Sam."

"Hazel."

"Don't do the thing where you just say my name instead of explaining yourself." I bite my lip and will myself not to cry again. I'm probably going to get my period any second, just to make this weekend extra-special. "What do you mean, you love me?"

"I can't stop thinking about you. I miss you, constantly. Work has been an unholy mess for months, and it doesn't touch me, because any time I pull out my phone, you've sent me something funny or sexy or sweet, and it makes my fucking day. I want to camp out on your couch and work in my sweatpants. I want—"

My heart explodes. He wants to spend more time with me. In sweatpants. "Can you do that?"

"Yeah."

"Do you own sweatpants?"

"I'll buy some. We can go to Walmart."

I don't think Sam has ever been to a suburban strip mall. This will be fun, like an anthropology field trip.

He rubs his thumb against the corner of my mouth. "What did you mean that you want more time?"

"More time together. I was thinking…" My heart thumps hard against my ribs. "I could stay at your place more often. During the week. And maybe on the weekend…"

"I'll come here." He kisses me again, hard this time, and he doesn't stop until I'm gasping and horny and really conflicted about the fact we're still in public, because I want to crawl up his body and do filthy things right freaking now. But then he keeps talking, and it's better than sex. "I've done a lot of stupid shit in my life, Hazel. I've wasted a lot of time being unhappy and making poor choices. I don't want to waste another chance to tell you how special you are to me. How happy you make me."

"Okay." I'm grinning now. "Can we go back to my place?"

"Hell yes." He tosses his bag over his shoulder, keeping his other arm wrapped tightly around me.

Once we're outside, he slides his hand down my arm, tangling our gloved fingers together. "I'm sorry you were upset this morning."

"Yeah." I turn my face to the weak winter sun. "I'm fine now. And I distracted myself with work."

"Tell me."

Two little words. Easy. Safe. Tell him my current story, tell him my fantasy. Weave a tale that gets him hard and leads to amazing sex.

"I've started writing a novel," I tell him instead. "It's complicated."

"All the best stories are."

"It's set in Toronto. It's about love and secrets and pain."

"I like it already."

"You like everything I write."

"That is true." He squeezes my hand. "Is this book about us?"

My eyelids flutter shut for a second. Big feelings. "Maybe a

little. Inspired by, but not directly ripped from the headlines."
I hesitate. "How overwhelming love is. How surprising."

He stops in the middle of the sidewalk, halfway to my wee little house. My tiny bungalow in my quiet small town.

Sam doesn't fit here. On this street, in my life. He's urban and expensive. Modern and polished.

And yet right now, right here... I blink.

I was so excited to see him before that I didn't *see* him.

He's wearing a new coat. A parka. Big, puffy, sensible. And on his feet are heavy boots. His perfect hair is still perfect, and I know his jeans didn't come from Walmart. But Sam is dressed for winter in the country.

I didn't notice.

"You got a new coat," I say dumbly.

"I want to spend more time here."

"You said that."

"Hazel—"

I grab his hand and pull him along. I need to be at home for this conversation. I need to be naked, probably. I'm ill-prepared for full and complete honesty.

Sam doesn't say anything else. He drops his bag in the hallway to my bedroom, then takes off his coat and boots and puts them next to mine at the front door. Coats hanging together get me all full of feels.

How surprising love is indeed.

I lead him straight to bed.

"I wrote us a story," I whisper as we undress each other. "About a young woman who is lost in a forest. A dark, forbidden forest. And a woodcutter finds her. She's scared and wet—it's been raining. It's cold. And he brings her back to his cabin."

There is no simple analogy for love. Nothing I've ever put down on the page is an exact match for how Sam makes me feel. But this story is close.

"What does he do to her?" Sam strokes his fingertips over my pretty bra, raising a line of goosebumps on my skin.

"He runs her a hot bath. Tells her to get into it and warm up, but when he leaves the room, she starts to cry."

Sam turns me around and slides the bra off my skin. "She's scared?"

I nod. "When he comes back into the washroom, she's just standing there. Little. Alone. Shivering. So he carefully undresses her, averting his eyes, and helps her into the hot water."

"Does he wash her back?"

"Not that night. She just sits in the tub until she warms up, and then he dries her off. Dresses her in some of his clothes and tucks her into bed. But the next night, she needs her hair washed. The night after that, she holds his hands as he dries her off."

He wraps his arms around me, his hands covering my breasts as he hugs me from behind. "Are they falling in love?"

I shake my head. "No. I mean, they will, of course. And there's an attraction. They want each other desperately, but they can't fall in love. Not yet. Because she has secrets. And maybe so does he."

"He'll tell her anything," Sam whispers in my ear. "He trusts her with all of his secrets."

"He has a dark past," I breathe. "Reasons for why he's all alone in the woods."

"And she'll be the only person who ever truly knows how he feels about those mistakes." Sam turns me around and picks me up, carrying me to my bed.

"She knows who he is." I curl up in a tight ball inside his arms, not wanting to let him go. "And she trusts him, anyway."

"He wants to be a different kind of man for her." He puts me down and joins me on the bed. He takes my chin between his fingers. "I want to be a different man for you. Now, and forever."

Oh, God. That word is just as scary as love. Forever.

I roll onto my back and stretch out. "I bought wood. For a fire."

He kisses my neck. "Will I pretend to have cut it down?"

"Yes please."

He laughs out loud, then rolls on top of me. "Deal."

"Sam?"

He smiles down at me. "Yes?"

"I love you, too."

"Thank God." He gives me his weight, and his mouth and, as I wrap my legs around him, a thickening cock, too.

We keep whispering woodcutter fantasy elements to each other as we fuck. It's slow and hot and fun. When I climax, my hair is wrapped around Sam's fist and his mouth is on my neck, growling obscenities that make me wet.

And once the aftershocks have finished rattling through both our bodies, his fingers are soft on my cheek, and his words are gentle.

Forever.

I couldn't imagine it. Not before. Not even this morning.

"What are you thinking?" he asks.

"That anything is possible." I kiss the soft curve of his lower lip, and he makes a happy noise. A cross between a murmur and a groan. "You know… I was wrong about the sounds I thought you'd make."

"Oh?"

"The sex sounds aren't the best ones. They're good, don't get me wrong. I love the grunt you make as you come."

"I do not."

Every single time, and it twists me inside out. "You do. But the sounds that really undo me are the secretly happy ones after sex. Like when I kiss you."

I do it again, and he makes the same murmur-groan.

"That."

"Ah," he whispers. "Those are Hazel-only sounds."

I close my eyes as he kisses me back and let myself sail straight into that unexpected joy. Hazel-only sounds.

How wonderful.

How perfectly, delightfully, unexpectedly wonderful.

18

SAM

I'M on my sixth Aibhlin Moon book. But this is the first time I've read one while holding the author.

She's asleep, and I'm up early. I could have crept downstairs and left her sleeping, but the way she confessed to bursting into tears when my train was late—well, I just want to hold her.

It amazes me that this soft, warm woman who has welcomed me into her bed also creates dark, twisted fantasies. It doesn't surprise me that Hazel is capable of that, of course. She's smart and observant. I've always known that, and noticed that she has no limits when it comes to sex.

But in the last two months, I've also fallen desperately in love with her sweetness, her kindness.

A sweet, kind, creative woman, who writes books about people's deepest, darkest fantasies.

This one is about a woman on the run, who has taken refuge with a dangerous man, and despite the implausible set-up, I'm deeply invested in both characters getting what they want and need.

So deeply invested, I don't notice Hazel waking up. She doesn't move, just quietly blinks her eyes open, which I only realize after the fact when she says, in a sleep-laden voice, "Oh, damn, there's a typo!"

I drop the book in surprise. "Morning," I say, kissing the top of her head. "And I wasn't reading it to catch errors. Wouldn't have noticed it even if you paid me."

"We do pay people to catch those," she mutters.

"I won't be applying for that job. I'm just a fan."

She buries her face in my shoulder. "Great."

"It is great." I haul her on top of me. "I love your words."

"All the boys say that," she says, laughing, but I don't think she's joking.

I tug her hair and pull her gaze to meet mine. "I'm not a boy."

"I know that."

I wait.

She looks away. Then looks back. "I *know* that. What we have is different. But I've built some pretty solid walls around this stuff."

"Tell me more about that."

"It's weird, okay? Dating and being an erotica writer at the same time."

"Men have been gross about it?"

"Sometimes. Sometimes not at first, but when I'm not exactly the same as…" She scrambles off my lap, putting a bit of distance between us, and gestures to the book. "I like some of the things I write about. But it's not like…it's not like that in real life, at least not for me."

"Tell me more." There's an edge to my voice, sharp and urgent, but it's nothing more than desire. I make eye contact with her. "Please."

"Have you read *For Her Own Good?*" She eyes me nervously.

I can picture it immediately, it has a birdcage on the cover. "Not yet, but I love that cover."

She waves her hand. "Don't read it."

I'm starting as soon as I get back to my apartment. "Why not?"

She covers her face, then mumbles. "No, you should read it. Yes. But with some warning, because I don't want you to get the wrong idea about me."

"I don't read your books as some kind of shortcut to understanding you as a woman." I frown, and reach for her. I need that contact, and when she folds into me, soft and cuddly, I know she does, too. "You don't think that's why I've been reading them, is it? I know you aren't your characters."

"Then why are you reading them?" It's a question she's never asked me before.

"Because you're a damn good writer." My voice catches. "Because they're hot, and they came from your imagination, but I know they're fiction. They're entertainment, and entertaining. I can't stop reading them when I get into one. That's why I keep picking them up. That's all."

"You don't want to know if I…" She trails off.

Oh, fuck yes. I want to know if she *anything*. But not because of a book. "If I have my way, we have the rest of our lives to figure out new and interesting ways to be dirty together."

She wraps her arms around me and buries her face in my neck.

I hug her back. Hard.

We have more to talk about there, obviously, but first... breakfast. "Can I make you some Eggs Benny?"

She nods, a tight bob constrained by the fact that I'm pinning her against me.

I'M BUILDING Hazel a perfect goat cheese and avocado Eggs Benny when she asks me the question, so it takes me a second to reply.

And in that second, she tries to take it back.

"Never mind, it's not—"

"No, say it again." I put down the pot of hollandaise sauce and grab a dish towel. She's got me curious now.

She licks her lips, her eyes wide. "Have you ever been to a sex club?"

"Nope." I hold my hand out, and she takes it. I tug her close. "Why do you ask?"

"Um..." Her breath goes funny as I stroke my fingertips against her collarbone. "Remember the bearded guy at Alex's house on New Year's Eve?"

"Mmm."

"He owns a sex club."

I stop my teasing touches. "Really." I say it like a statement, but it's a question, too. *How do you know?*

Hazel laughs, answering the unspoken part. "I follow him online. For research. I've never been, but...I would. If you would."

I grab her plate and set it on the table. "Sit."

She sits.

I quickly assemble a plate for myself, taking zero care in the details. "Sure, if you want to go, I'd go with you. Do you want me to ask Alex about it? He loves to introduce people."

"I noticed." She's looking at me like I'm not getting it.

That's because I'm not getting. "What is the missing puzzle piece here?"

"Is Alex kinky?"

"Jesus." I laugh. Then I gesture at the eggs. "I just wanted to make brunch."

"Sorry, not sorry."

"No need to be sorry." I think about it. "Maybe? If he is, he's discreet about it. But even if he knows that guy through another channel, he'd still make the introduction."

She takes a bite of her eggs, then another. Then she puts her fork down with a clatter. "Or we could just go. It's not a closed club, anyone can go. You just have to sign a waiver around privacy and let them take a photo of your driver's license."

"You've done your research."

Hazel looks uncharacteristically shy. "Yes. But it's not just research. I mean, it always has been. In the past, when it's come up with men I've dated, I have always segmented kink off as work, as research, because every time I bring it up, it winds being…complicated. Good, at first, but then bad. Very bad." She gives me a hard-to-read-look. "And there are some echoes from the past, between us, of you liking me because I'm dirty."

Well, that's direct. "I like that you're dirty. Sure. Okay. But I love you because you're straight with me. That you hold me to a higher standard than the jackass I once was."

Her eyes widen again. She's not the only one who can be direct.

"Let's eat," I say again. "Do you want me to feed you?"

She laughs. Our knees bump as we dig into the food, and after a few bites, she reaches out and tangles her fingers around my free hand. "This is really good. The food, the company. The relationship. What we have is really good."

"I agree."

"So I want to say that I haven't been keeping anything from you, not exactly, but I have maybe tried to temper what I say out loud versus maybe what's in my head. But there have been a few times when the world I write in has bumped up against what we have here, and I guess it's time to talk about that more fully."

Fuck, yeah. I'm all ears. "Shoot. What's in your head?"

"Lots of things. Pain and…bondage."

My cock twitches eagerly. "Okay. Yes, please."

She laughs. "But there are right ways to do it. Safety considerations."

I frown. "Has anyone ever hurt you?"

"Eh, maybe. Nothing bad, but some stupid shit. Rope burn

once, and a bit of a panic-inducing couldn't-get-a-knot-undone situation. That was the end of that exploration outside my head."

"I'll learn whatever needs to be learned." I squeeze her hand, but that's not enough. I haul her into my lap, the table jostling because I'm too big and too rough, but only with it. Never with Hazel, unless she wants me to be.

She straddles me, our breakfast forgotten momentarily, and I kiss her.

"Whatever you want," I promise against her lips. "Because you're mine. And I love all of you. Your sweetness, your cleverness, and your darkest thoughts, too."

"They're not that dark," she giggles. "But maybe a little depraved?"

I groan. "I'll be the judge of that."

WE EVENTUALLY FINISH EATING, but as soon as the dishes are cleared, I'm on her again. I pin her against the counter and kiss the back of her neck. "Did you have any other plans for the day?"

"Other than telling you about my kinkiest desires?" Hazel clears her throat. "I thought maybe we could go shopping for a new porch light."

I ease my hands under her shirt, making her shiver. "I'm at your service."

"I like being trapped," she whispered. "Here, against the counter. And when you pin me down in bed."

"I've noticed that. I like it, too."

"You could be rougher."

My cock agrees. I press against her at the same time as I tighten my grip on her side, just below her bare breast. "Yeah?"

A wordless nod.

"I don't want to hurt you."

"You won't. You're going to make me feel good."

"Tell me how it'll feel good. Help me understand so I can get it right."

Her eyes light up. "I think it's like having your back scratched, that sensation on the skin. Sometimes sex is so… mouth, tits, pussy focused. But what if my entire skin was a sex organ?"

"You think…what if…" I grab a hold on her, my hands hard and big on her hips. I cover as much of her beautiful, sensitive skin as I can get my fingers on. I skate my hands down her thighs, then back up and onto her torso. When I squeeze her tight just below the breasts, she shudders. "Hazel, haven't you played at this before?"

"Not really."

I drag my hands up and over her breasts, roughly, then back again. Soft now. I know how to touch a woman all over, but she wants more than that. "I want to make you feel as good as you possibly can."

"I know." She smiles at me, a brilliant, trusting beam of light. "That's why I asked."

"You're my captive, then." I bite the side of her neck. "Mine to bite and maul…"

She makes a happy sound. "Yes, please."

"Do you like that? A bit of pain?"

"Yes." She rakes her lower lip between her teeth. "Maybe more than a little? But I haven't…"

It's heady, knowing she's sharing this fully with me first. "Let's try."

She whimpers. Holy fuck.

"Can I pinch you?"

"Yes," she breathes.

"Do you want it to hurt?"

She gasps. "Yes."

"A little or a lot?"

"A little." A dreamy smile curls at the corners of her mouth. "Please."

"So polite," I whisper. Then I clamp my fingers together, just enough to push into her soft, tender flesh.

Another gasp, this one longer, sustained, and it comes with a look of beautiful wonder on her face.

I hold her skin between my fingers, marvelling at the connection between that sharpness and her pleasure, then I release. She shudders, a full body ripple effect. When I slide my hand the last inch up her thigh, I find her slit swollen and dripping.

"You liked that?"

She nods eagerly.

I kiss her roughly. "Good," I growl against her mouth. "So did I."

19

HAZEL

I'm on fire. I need Sam inside me, now. But when I open my mouth, all that comes out are mewling pleas.

"I've got you." He hoists me up on the counter, pushing my t-shirt up my hips. Baring my wet slit.

I gasp his name and he pinches me again, this time on the inside of my thigh. My head spins. My clit throbs.

"Yes?"

"Oh God." I nod. *Yes, a million times yes.*

"Look how hard you make me," he growls as he pushes his shorts down. His cock bobs into the space between my legs, dark at the tip and bigger than I've ever seen it before. "I'm going to enjoy hurting you, Hazel."

Holy shit. I moan, and he shoves into me, not taking any time to get me used to the heavy thickness of him. Demanding space inside me, forcing me to take it.

I grab at his shoulders, holding on for dear life as he fucks me, his hands hard on my hips. Pinning me in place.

His captive.

His dirty sex captive. His wet, willing captive. My mind riots, an out-of-control celebration of yes, this, finally.

Him, finally.

Need grips me, harder than Sam is holding me down, and I buck against him, against that powerful pull inside me. The more I fight it, the hotter I get, the more intense the feeling builds, until it's on top of me.

I shatter into a million pieces as Sam grunts that he's coming, too, inside me, whether I like it or not, and I like it so fucking much I start laughing.

"I love you," I whisper against his damp skin.

He grips me tight and squeezes. "I love you, too."

"That was really hot."

He helps me down. "All right, wild woman. I can do better."

I laugh again, blissed out and pleased more than he could ever imagine. "Race you to the shower."

AN HOUR LATER, we're at the hardware store, looking at lights. I took photos of the fixture I have, but we can't find one that will replace it exactly. The ones I like the most are a completely different shape, and the wiring isn't the same.

I frown at the instructions on the side of the box. "This seems complicated. Maybe I should probably hire an electrician to install it."

Sam doesn't look concerned. "We can do that ourselves."

"I really don't think we can."

"Sure, it's easy. We just need to turn off the main power supply, then follow the step-by-step instructions. As long as you have a drill—"

"I do not."

"Oh."

"Should I?"

"Well, no…" He frowns. "If you don't want one. But they're fun."

"Do you have power tools?"

"I have a drill, and I use it as if I own an entire fleet of power tools."

"Then maybe I want a drill, too."

We cruise the aisles, Sam proud as a peacock that he can tell me the difference between an impact drill and a regular one, and why it's not a bad idea to get both in a set, just in case.

But it's when we get to the tool belt section that I really get excited about this little adventure. "You should get one of these. To wear the drill in between…drillings."

"You like that?" He grins and grabs a basic black nylon option. A heady, horny thrill zings through me.

But I have a specific fantasy in mind, so I shake my head and point to the classic leather one. "That one. I'll find something for you to fix as often as you want to wear it for me."

"Yeah?" His eyes are hot now, laser-focused on my face. The zinging gets better and worse at the same time.

It's definitely heating up in aisle six, and that's probably not appropriate.

But I don't really give a damn about appropriate.

"Please," I whisper.

The corner of his mouth crooks up, a soft little tell in an otherwise burning-hot expression. "Since you ask so nicely," he growls. "But this project might get more detailed than I first quoted. I hope you're able to pay the full bill for this house call, ma'am."

I definitely will not be able to pay the full bill. "And if I can't?"

His gaze flashes greedily. "We'll figure something out." He glances around. "Now, do you think they sell rope in this place?"

"What?" I heard him just fine. I know why he's asking. But that's going from zero to sixty, and…I like it. I love it. "Sam, are you serious?"

"That's what you meant by bondage, right?" He flashes a devastating grin. "If we buy with all this other stuff, they're not going to think it's for anything dirty, right?"

"This is my local hardware store!"

"Okay, I'll check out on my own." He leans in and kisses me. "You can scurry out front and be quietly mortified. I think that's kind of hot."

"I've created a monster."

I get another kiss for that. "Maybe. Let's go look at rope."

BACK AT MY HOUSE, Sam silently unloads his purchases. The fancy new drill, the light we're going to install, the tool belt, two different kinds of cotton rope, and a terrifyingly large pair of shears.

"For safety," he said as he plucked it off the shelf.

I spontaneously combusted.

Now I'm hovering next to him, a re-assembled collection of horny pieces.

He grabs the tool belt first and straps it on. "All right, let's get to work. Can you go and turn off the main power?"

"But what about the rope?" I blurt out.

He glances at it casually. "That's for later. After I do some research of my own. Let's talk about it—after you kill the main power."

"Bossy."

"Is that something you like?"

"Only when I'm tied up, I'm pretty sure," I lob back.

His grin is so broad, it fills me with joy, and I scamper down to the basement to turn off the breaker panel.

It's cold outside, and my fingers get stiff immediately, but Sam doesn't seem to mind. He smoothly removes the old light, then follows the instructions to get the new one installed. Before I know it, he's sending me back downstairs to turn the power on, and we haven't talked about rope play at all.

When I return, the new light is in place—shiny and new, and much more substantial. Fitting to the era of my home. "I love it." I clap my hands. "But I don't have any money to pay you."

"Well, that's going to be a problem," he says, drawing out

each word with extra-serious emphasis. "Let's step inside and discuss your options."

"Options?" I open the door and he pushes up against me, shoving me in a little.

"I did a job for you, ma'am. It's only fair I get something in return." He glances at the rope on the ottoman. "Or…"

"Or?" I sound way too eager.

He shrugs. "I wouldn't want to have to tie you up. Make sure you don't go anywhere."

"Oh," I breathe. "Well…"

He gestures at the tool belt, framing a denim-bound erection. "Options, ma'am. You could distract me with that pretty little mouth. It looks nice and soft. Wet."

My belly quivers. "You want my mouth?"

He racks his gaze down my body. "To start."

"And if I say no?"

His gaze darkens to a scary glower. *Yes, please.* "You don't want to say no."

"But I can't…" I whisper it, licking my lips. "I can't let you have my mouth."

"Just remember, I gave you that option." He grabs me roughly and peels off my coat, then shoves off his own.

"Wait," I whisper.

He freezes, his hands gentling on my arms.

"Just lock the door first."

He stifles a laugh as he twists and flips the deadbolt. Then he shoves me into the living room, where I stumble into the couch as he carefully draws the drapes fully closed.

He grabs a bundle of rope and approaches me, looming

large. "Here's the thing, ma'am." He sighs and uncoils the rope, letting it fall on me in a loose pile. "I like you. I like doing work for you. But a man deserves compensation, you know. And if you don't have money for me, and you won't give me anything else freely, then I'll need to take it."

"Please don't," I whisper.

And Sam, because he is lovely, stops again. Looks at me. Really looks. We should have talked about this first, we both know that, but fuck it.

I smile. "Please don't take it. But if you tie me up, then I can give you what you want. Just so long as I have that cover...should I be discovered. I can't be known as a loose woman, you see."

"Don't worry." He roughly rubs his thumb against my lower lip, making my mouth fall open. "This will be our little secret. Yes, like that. Lick me. Show me what that little mouth can do when you don't have any other choice."

I suck at his thumb eagerly, and moan when he pulls away.

He grabs my hands and presses my wrists together, wrapping them swiftly in the rope. He doesn't make it too tight, and he coils the rope up my forearms, spreading the pressure away from just my wrists.

It feels remarkable. Like a hug. Firm but not hard, restrictive but not too much.

"Are you all right?" His voice changes, just Sam now, just for a second, and I meet his gaze.

I nod. "Perfect."

"I knew it," he drawls, back in character. "Just needed to be shown you didn't have a choice in the matter." He notches his thumbs against the tool belt, his fingers pressing against the imprint of his cock behind his fly. "I like the way you look like this."

I swallow hard.

He takes his time unzipping, palming himself first through his jeans, and then inside, keeping his cock hidden from my hungry view.

By the time he shoves his boxers down and fists his bare cock in front of my face, I'm panting. I swallow him eagerly, the fact I can't touch him at all a wild limit that jacks up my arousal. It makes me squirm on the couch, press my thighs together.

Sam notices. "You like that, huh? My big cock in your mouth, nothing to stop me. You're so pretty like this, with your lips stretched wide, and your hands tied up like that. Look at me, Hazel. Look at how much I like this, too."

I nod up at him, making a fumbling sound around his erection. His eyes hood a bit more, his own mouth looking wet and slutty, just like mine.

I'm glad I told you, I try to say with my eyes.

He grins, a half-cocked smile that makes my insides flip. "This is so nice," he murmurs. "But I don't want to come like this."

I squeak as he pulls out.

"I want to see if you like it, too."

It's harder than it sounds for him to push me back and strip my jeans off me while my hands are tied and in the way, but then he lifts my arms, resting the rope-bound limbs against my head—and baring my body to him.

I'm tied up and stretched out on the couch while a handyman violates me, and it's everything I thought it would be and more.

It's silly and hot and unexpected.

His hand feels extra-big and extra-rough as he pushes my thighs apart.

I close my eyes as I picture what he's looking at, my pink pussy, wet and shiny in the afternoon winter light streaming in from the kitchen.

It's quiet in my house, and I'm suddenly aware of his breathing. A little laboured, a lot aroused.

My clit throbs under his appraisal, I can feel it twitch, and he groans. He saw it, too. He was looking at me that closely.

Then I feel his mouth on me, warm and hungry. His tongue moves over my flesh, not missing an inch. He fucks it into me, uses it to nudge my clit, too. Then he sucks. My legs start to shake, desperate trembles, and I rock my hips, eager for more.

But just like my mouth on his cock, this isn't how he wants it to end.

With a grunt, he grabs my arms and releases the rope. "Oh," I gasp as my shoulders sag free. I hadn't realized how tight I was holding my arms.

Sam rubs my wrists, then flips me over. "Just pretend you're still bound," he growls in my ear as he covers me, as his heavy cock finds my cunt slick and ready. "Just pretend you don't have a choice, that I'm taking this as my payment. But we both know you want it. We both know you have money to pay me, and you're hiding it somewhere in this house."

"Ah!" I gasp and shove back against him, my hips rocking independently now. Fuck, fuck, yes.

"Need you like this."

"Yes."

"Say it."

"I need you, too. Like this. Rough. I need it." I keep whispering those three words, *I need it I need it I need it* as the tool belt digs into my hips, pressing hard, as his cock drags in and out of my sensitive folds. I'll be sore by the end of the day at this rate.

I can't wait.

"Make me come," I mumble into the couch cushion.

I don't know if he hears me, but it doesn't matter. The mental picture of him looming behind me, both of us still partially dressed, gets me there. I shove one hand under my body to find my clit, and I go flying as soon as my fingertip makes contact.

A groan rips from my chest, and behind me, Sam echoes it as he buries himself deep inside me.

My beloved, keeper of my secrets and my sounds.

20

SAM

"WHAT ELSE SHOULD I read up on?"

"Sam!"

I grin at Hazel. We're standing in the middle of the train station, saying a lingering goodbye because the train is a few minutes late. I don't mind it when it buys us a little more time. "Come on. Give me something to think about on the trip home."

She bites her lower lip, glances left and right, then leans in and lowers her voice. "I want to be spanked. For real."

"Like punishment?"

"Like a reward."

"Fascinating." My pulse thumps heavy in my veins. "I can't wait for next weekend."

"Same." She kisses me full on the mouth, a soft promise that our time apart will be full of research.

To that end, as soon as I'm on the train, I text Alex, giving him a two-hour heads-up that I'm about to appear on his doorstep. I get off the train and get right on the subway, going straight to his place before I even go home.

He gives my backpack the once over. "Are you coming or going?"

"Just got home from a weekend in the country."

"Hazel is still tolerating your presence?"

I can't deny the truth there. "I remain confused about her attachment to me as well, but I'm doing my best to be a good companion. Which is why I'm here."

"Your mysterious and urgent request for an audience." He sweeps his hand into the gloomy foyer. "Come on in. Do you want coffee?"

"Sure." I follow him into the kitchen.

"What's the urgent issue we need to discuss?"

"My girlfriend recognized someone at your party. I would like an introduction."

"Of course. Who was it?"

"Zeke Devereaux."

Alex's expression doesn't change. "Okay."

"You aren't curious why?"

"No."

"Why not?"

"Because she writes erotica and Zeke owns a kink club."

"Right."

Alex's expression changes then, from careful acknowledgment to naked curiosity. "Unless it's more than research."

"No, it's research."

"Hands on research?"

"Are you asking as a nosy friend?"

The corners of his mouth twitch. "Not exactly. Asking more as Zeke's silent partner in the club."

"What?" I rub my hand over my mouth. "Wow, you think you know someone..."

"You know me just fine. I don't think you want the ins and outs of how people have sex."

"No."

"Right."

"Good."

"Okay." He shrugs. "I'll set it up. Zeke's a good guy. His wife is one of my favourite people in this world, but she doesn't care for my mixed-company parties. Zeke doesn't usually come, either, but I wanted him to meet someone."

"Who?"

Alex shakes his head. "That's not for me to share." He crosses to an oversized apothecary chest against the far wall, unlocks it, and pulls a business card from a drawer. "Here. This is a pass for two to a VIP night. Each weekend, one night is open to the public, and one night is reserved for people with that card. It's a different vibe. Zeke and Caro are committed to being public facing and educating people on doing kink safely, responsibly, but it's better when you know nobody is there to gawk."

I take it and thank him. "Hazel wanted to go to the public night."

"They're fun, too. But these nights are better."

"Do you...go to them?"

"Rarely. You won't see me there, don't worry. I put the

silent in silent partner. I only show up when summoned by Caro."

I nod. "Hey, another question. For research purposes. Do you have any preferred websites or books about rope stuff?"

THE NEXT NIGHT I'm on the phone with Hazel when there's a knock at my apartment door. Since only a handful of people can get past the doorman without a call up to me, I open it while I'm still talking.

It's Grace, and I wave her in. *Hazel*, I mouth as I point to the phone. She has a takeout bag in her hand, and she waves it toward the kitchen.

Belatedly, I realize I left the VIP card for The Wheelhouse on the counter in there, and I race after her.

In my ear, Hazel is talking about other home improvement projects we could do together, and I have to cut her off. "Sweetheart, I need to go. I'll call you right back."

"Sure. Is everything okay?"

I look at Grace, holding the card, and groan. "Yep, totally fine. It's just Grace nosing in my private business. Give me five minutes to kick her out and then I'm all yours again."

Grace is laughing at me as I put the phone on the counter where the card just was. "You didn't need to end the call on my account."

"What are you doing here?"

"Feeding you."

"I have food."

"Feeding myself in your presence because Luke is working late, and I was lonely, then."

"Ah." I glance at the phone.

"Call her back. I don't care if you're busy, I just like the hum of another person in my space."

I frown.

Grace doesn't notice. She's still chuckling at the card. "The Wheelhouse, eh? I wouldn't have pegged you for the type."

"You can't do this," I burst out.

She drops the card, startled.

"I know you mean well, and I love you for it, but…I was talking to my girlfriend. That card…is because I want to go there with my girlfriend. You can't just waltz into my house and make this awkward for me!"

She takes a step back, then nods. "Of course."

"Grace…"

"No, I get it. I'll take my food and go to the studio instead. There are usually people there all night."

I feel like shit. "I've gone about this poorly."

"Probably," she says, her voice a bit sad, because of fucking course it is, I just yelled at her. "But is there a right way to remind someone they're tromping on boundaries? Maybe not. It's fine. I'll go, and I'll text next time I'm looking for dinner company."

She grabs the takeaway bag, which smells really good, and swings past me, patting me on the arm on her way out.

Fucking hell.

As the door clicks shut behind her, I pick up my phone and call Hazel back.

"Hey," I mutter when she answers.

"Oh, no."

"I yelled at Grace. And she knows I have a card for The Wheelhouse."

Hazel laughs. "I'm sorry, that sucks all around."

"I might go after her, walk her to the studio. That's where she said she's going."

"Okay. Text me when you get home."

"I love you."

"Me, too. Go make it right."

I catch up to Grace as she's getting in her car, parked halfway down the street. "Wait," I shout out.

She stops and looks back. The way her face brightens up slays me. My brother is a fucking tool.

"I'm sorry, I reacted badly. Do you want to come back upstairs? Or do you want company at the studio?"

She presses her lips together, then tilts her head to the side. "Actually, I want to show you something. If you're game?"

INSTEAD OF CROSSING under the freeway, Grace points her car toward the fashion district. After heading east, then zipping down a narrow side street, she turns on Richmond and parks in front of an art gallery.

"I'm going to have a show here next month," she says. "I told Luke about it today, and he said, and I quote, 'As long as my name isn't attached to it.' Can you believe him?"

"I'm sorry."

"Yeah. Me, too." She sighs and turns the car off. "Come on. I have a key."

After letting us in, and punching in the security code to re-arm the door, she leads me through the current exhibit to a door, which leads to a back room. When she flicks on the lights, blinding whiteness fills the space. It takes a minute for my eyes to adjust, and when they do, I realize I'm not just looking at Grace's work. I immediately recognize a couple of her sculptures, lush, feminine bodies, but there are paintings, too, of angular bodies in embrace. And at the far end of the room is an overwhelming tangle of harsh metal.

It takes me another minute to figure out what I'm looking at, because all the art pieces are jammed together in this staging room. In the middle of the tangle is a birdcage almost as tall as the space.

A birdcage just like on the cover of Hazel's book.

I turn back to Grace and her pieces. "This is…a joint show? Next month?"

She nods, clearly proud—as she should be. "Alex put me in touch with a local patron, who was already helping the other two artists get this show off the ground. When Alex mentioned that I used to work in the gallery world, and might have a few pieces I could contribute, I…well, I jumped into the deep end. I didn't know I wanted this. I thought my online business was enough, but there's nothing quite like a show, Sam. I'm…"

"And then Luke shit all over it."

"Yeah."

"And then I yelled at you for interrupting my phone date."

She laughs weakly. "Yes. But I think you were more embarrassed that I saw the VIP night card, right?"

I force myself not to look away. "Yeah, probably."

"That's why I wanted to show you this. It's Deke—the owner—who Alex wanted me to meet. So if you have the VIP card, you should know that you might see my work at his club. And…you might see me, there, too."

My mouth drops open.

"That's a secret," she says, her voice tight. "From your brother, too."

"Grace…"

"I'm not doing anything wrong." She turns away. "I just didn't want you to be surprised. That's all."

"I don't know what to say."

"You don't need to say anything. Just hear it, and then… you know, in time."

I'm the last person to offer relationship advice or judge someone for their choices. "I'm proud of you. I know that much."

She glances back over her shoulder. "Thanks."

"And I'm starving. Can we eat?"

"Of course." She pulls a canvas drop cloth off a sculpture and sets it on the ground. "Do you mind having a picnic on the floor?"

"No." I frown at the sculpture. "Is this yours?"

Her brow pulls tight. "Yeah."

"It's not a woman."

"I branch out sometimes."

It's a man, head ducked low. No face visible, because his heavy body is twisted away. And there's a pair of hands on his back. Soft, small hands.

Something stops me from asking more about it, so I sit and eat with her. But the first thing I do when I get home is look up her website, where she keeps a catalogue of all of her work.

And my heart sinks.

SAM DOESN'T CALL me back for a few hours, and when he does, he sounds weary.

"Luke's not proud of her," he says, and my heart breaks.

"That's awful."

"I think she's checked out of their relationship, which may be for the best. For her, anyway. But I think it's going to get messy before it gets better. This is her first big public show, and one of the pieces for it is called *Death of a Marriage*."

"Oh." I want to throw reassurance at him, remind him that art doesn't always reflect life, and that's a common theme for creators to tangle with. But Sam knows this couple better than anyone. If he is worried, I'm not going to minimize that fear. "I'm sorry. For them, and you. That's a lot of stress to carry."

"Yeah."

"Does it feel better to talk about it?"

"I don't know."

"Do you want me to distract you?"

He chuckles in my ear. "Yes."

So I tell him about what I'm currently working on, and how I'm looking forward to the weekend, and we don't talk about his family again that night.

I CATCH the first train Friday morning, and Sam meets me at the train station. He's dressed in his Bay Street uniform, an expensive suit, with his hair slicked back.

We probably make a funny pair, me in my yoga pants and hiking boots, a backpack tossed over my shoulder, enthusiastically kissing a business shark.

"I have time to run you to my place before my next meeting," he says, tucking me tight into his side as we navigate the hustle and bustle. "And then I'll be back for dinner. Sound good?"

"Sounds great." I exhale a breath I hadn't realized I'd been holding.

He squeezes me tight, like he noticed, and I press my head in his body.

"Hey, I've been doing some research," he murmurs once we're in the back of a cab.

I turn my head so I can murmur right back. "About what?"

"Rope."

"Interesting."

"Some people find that being tied up helps with anxious feelings."

I laugh. "Are you going to tie me to your bed while you're at work?"

"That would hardly be safe." He sets his hand on my back, just below my neck. "But what about wearing a rope halter?"

I blink in surprise. "That's some pretty good research."

"You know about them?"

"Yeah."

"Good." He kisses my temple. "You've got ten minutes to decide if you want one for the afternoon."

I don't have to think about it.

I'm vibrating with excitement when we get upstairs. Sam is very cute about it. He's watched YouTube videos, he explains, but he wants to watch them while he's doing it. "Is that okay? Does it take some of the fun out of it?"

"Not at all." I feel lighter than air, knowing he's going to do this and he cares about getting it right, and I tell him that. "Do your thing."

He has the same rope he bought and left at my place. I try to picture him making a hardware store run in his suit, those polished shoes, and I start giggling.

Sam catches my face in his and kisses me, swallowing my laughter. Turns it to soft moans. Then he spins me around and gets to work. The rope is doubled, and the pressure feels so nice as he pulls it around me. Up and over my shoulders, down between my breasts. He's putting the harness on over my shirt, but each brush of his fingertips against my skin, even through the fabric, makes me sizzle.

"There you go," he says as he tucks the ends neatly away. "And if it bothers you at any point, you can cut yourself out of it. But if you're still in it when I get home, I'll untie you, and you can tell me how it felt to be bound like this all day."

After he leaves, I move through his loft enjoying the feel of the rope gently hugging my body. I look at it in the mirror in his bathroom, slide my fingers against the double strands, the loops where they split and twist.

Then I dig out my laptop and get set up to work on his bed, with that million dollar view out the window.

Hours pass, and I'm startled to realize the sun is setting. I unfurl myself from the nest of pillows and blankets I was writing in and head into the main open space to think about dinner.

One of the paintings on the wall catches my eye, an abstract.

That's where Sam finds me.

He crosses to me and tugs at the back of the harness, spinning me around so he can kiss me deeply. "Missed you all day."

I smile against his mouth. "I didn't miss you, because I had you all around me."

He groans. "Fuck, I love that."

"Me, too."

"So this felt good?"

"Yep."

"Can I take it off you now?" When I nod, he steps back, takes off his jacket, and rolls up his sleeves to his elbows. Then he reaches for my harness, and slowly reverses the careful steps he took earlier.

I roll my shoulders as he sets the coil down, then he tells me to lift my arms, and he peels off my shirt.

Underneath are faint rope marks, and he leans in to kiss one shoulder, then the other. I shiver at the touch, not realizing how sensitive the skin had become until he brushed his lips against the mark.

He lifts his head, frowning. "Okay?"

"Better than okay." I try to capture what it feels like. "I feel all loose and relaxed, and skin-prickly sensitive at the same time."

He gently wraps me in his arms, then points to the painting. "You were deep in thought when I came in."

"Is this one of Grace's?"

"No. But she bought it for me. Why?"

"I don't know. Just wondering. Maybe I should spend more time with her. Get to know her?"

"She would love that."

"Would you?"

He frowns. "Of course. Why?"

"That relationship seems complicated."

"That's more about my brother, not her. Grace is the sister I wish I'd had. And yes, it's sometimes tense, but in a family kind of way."

"Can I ask…" I wince. "She's artsy. Different from you—and Luke."

He nods.

"And I'm…artsy. Different from you."

Another nod, but this time the muscles around his mouth twitch, tighten, and his lips narrow.

I just spill it out. "Is there any part of you that was in love with your sister-in-law? Am I a stand-in for her? Are you attracted to me because I'm…like her?"

Sam stares at me. Silent. Disbelieving, maybe.

Then he laughs. "No. Oh, no. God. No."

"Is that ridiculous? I don't know where that came from." I rub my chest, where the ropes were. "I haven't been worried about it."

"It's fine. You have it all wrong, though. Or not wrong, but backwards. Yes, you're a lot like Grace. *She's a lot like you.* I have always liked her, in part because she reminds me of you. I love her, yes, but I am not in love with her, and I never have been. That is reserved for you. And I think maybe it always has been."

My face goes hot with shame. "I'm sorry."

"Don't be. It needed to be aired. Is it done now?" He grins. "Do you have any other questions about who I might have feelings for?"

"No." It's a small word, mouthed by a small person. I should never have voiced that fear out loud. It was probably hurtful, even if he brushes it off, and I know better. Jealousy can bubble in the most unexpected, illogical ways, and needs to be dealt with logically. Snuffed out, given no oxygen.

Sam frowns. "I think I should tell you something. It's about my childhood, and it's not an excuse for anything, so I don't ever bring it up. But it's time you know. I would never, ever violate the trust you put in me, because I'm a product of exactly that kind of violation."

"What do you mean?"

"Luke and I don't look alike. I'm dark, he's light. He's heavier set than I am. He had freckles as a kid, and I tanned easily."

"What are you saying?"

His jaw flexes. "Neither of us look like our father, either."

"Oh, Sam."

He stalks away from the painting and throws himself onto the couch. "How much do you know about my family?"

I shake my head as I follow him. I perch close, but not too close. I'm here, but I don't know what I've done, opening this can of worms. I don't know if he needs space. "Not much. I know your parents are wealthy."

He nods, his mouth twisting hard into a grimace. "The thing about dynastic wealth is that you need heirs. Thirty-five years ago, my father made a deal with the devil when he turned a blind eye to my mother's first pregnancy. He convinced himself it was something he could live with."

"Luke."

Another nod. "It turned out, it wasn't the first pregnancy that destroyed our cozy family unit. It was the second. When I came out looking exactly like his best friend, and nothing like my brother. He never forgave me for that."

"That's fucked up." I blurt out my reaction. "Sam, that's not fair."

"Oh, I'm aware."

"I'm so sorry."

"Yeah." He gestures around. "It's why, when I ruined our business, they were not inclined to help us out. It's why you will likely never meet them. We don't have a relationship."

"Not even your mother?" I can't imagine. And I feel horribly inadequate in supporting him through this.

He groans and makes another face. "So you can see why I'm so attached to Grace. It's not love, not like that. It's that she's the only person who has ever loved me as a family member."

No. I'm crying now, wet, helpless drops sliding down my face.

He smiles at me. "Until you. And this...what we have...it's even better."

I throw myself at him, the lingering rope marks on my torso tender reminders of just how much I love and trust him.

He should be able to trust me, too.

On Monday, when Sam goes to work, I go to the Waterfront Centre and find Grace. I knock at the door of her studio, and it takes a minute for her to open the door.

"Hazel!" She looks surprised, but she steps back and gestures for me to enter.

"I hope I'm not disturbing you?"

"No, not at all. I love company." She gestures at the space. "Can I give you a quick tour? This is my sculpture work, here, but today I'm trying to paint. It's not going that well."

"I think it's all amazing," I promise her. "Listen, this is a bit awkward... but I owe you an apology."

"For what?"

"For thinking Sam was maybe in love with you." I wince. It sounds ridiculous when I say it out loud.

Her face softens. "I wish. And no, not because I'm in love with him. I'm hopelessly in love with his brother. But Sam is…he's done the work. He's a good catch." She tilts her head to the side. "Why did you want to tell me that?"

"Sam and I talked about it. And he told me about his family. I know how much he dislikes secrets, and how much he values you. I wanted to clear the air, because I love him more than I ever thought possible."

"He feels the same way, I can see it." She brushes her hand against her cheek, leaving a smear of paint.

When I point it out, she laughs. "I'm a mediocre painter, you know that? All of my pieces that have sold well have been sculpture. But I keep trying to make this good. I want to be good at *this*, and it frustrates me that I'm not."

"That's me and poetry." I reach into my bag and pull out the book I brought with me. "Speaking of which. Here. This is for you."

She stops moving—and it's only then that I realize she was moving the whole time. Her stillness is jarring, different. New. Then she inhales, sharply, and crosses to a sink on the wall. She takes her time washing her hands, then drying them, and the care in both actions hits me straight in the chest.

I came here to apologize, and she's treating my book—that few people in the world have ever cared about—with the utmost honour.

"It's really fine," I mutter. "It's just a chapbook."

She takes it and runs her finger over my pen name. "This is you?"

"Yep." It's my first poetry collection. Twenty-four pages, a narrow little bundle of dreams. "One of them is about Sam."

She presses it to her chest. "I love that."

Me, too. "Now you have a bit of my work. Proof that I've been in the muck?"

She laughs. "I think that proof was when you showed up. It was a very un-Preston thing to do."

"To confess my weaknesses?"

Her eyebrows raise in acknowledgement, even as she tries to keep her face straight. Tries and fails. "Yes."

"We're all imperfect and just doing our best."

Her face falls, just for a second, then she fixes a smile in place instead. In that moment, I understand Sam's protectiveness towards her.

"Grace, I'm in town all week. Do you want to have lunch one day? Or...many days? I liked the walk over here."

22

SAM

OVER DINNER THAT NIGHT, Hazel tells me she has decided not to go back to Stratford mid-week. "If you're going to come and work remotely for a week or two, I might hang out here until you're ready to come back with me."

"That's great. What made you change your mind?"

"I went to see Grace today. I want to spend more time with her, and you, here. When you come to my house, it's an escape. But I don't want to just help you escape. I want to be with you here, in the mess of real life."

I glance around my rather nice loft.

"You know what I mean!" She laughs.

"I do. And I appreciate it. In fact, as a thank you, I was wondering if you had another fantasy you might want me to indulge. I'll give you whatever you want."

Her eyes light up. "Really?"

As if it's any kind of hardship. "Oh, yeah."

"I have a lot of Sam fantasies."

"Name them."

She sits up a little straighter. "Can I be your secretary for a day?"

I swear under my breath, because that's so hot and how does she still surprise me? Endlessly. "Yes," I say hoarsely. "How does Saturday sound?"

23

HAZEL

BEFORE SAM LEAVES for the office on Saturday morning, he puts me in a harness. I'll wear it under my clothes this time. I stand in front of him in a bra and panties, the same scraps-of-nothing set he liked so much on New Year's Eve. He binds me in a new rope he ordered, one that's thin enough not to be noticed by random people.

His office should be empty, he says, but you never know.

I like that idea a lot.

After he leaves, I get dressed in an outfit I bought yesterday. Tight skirt. Not short. All the way to the knees, but if Sam wants to rip it, that's fine. I'm packing yoga pants I can change into for the trip home.

A white blouse and a grey cardigan complete the outfit.

I take the streetcar to Bay, just like a temp worker would. When I arrive at his building, I follow his instructions precisely, using the pass card he left for me to get into the elevator. His firm occupies the twenty-second floor, and when I step out of the elevator, the office is quiet, but the lights are on.

This is where his instructions end.

I'm not sure where I'm going next, so I head to the right. Looking for a corner office, maybe. I don't find Sam, so I turn around—and he's standing at the end of the hallway.

"Can I help you?"

"I'm here from the temp agency," I say demurely. "Hazel McLaughlin."

He gestures for me to come closer. "I'm one of the partners here. I called for a temp an hour ago. You're late."

"I'm sorry, sir."

"It's fine, but I have a conference call in ten minutes. Come along."

When he turns and stalks off, I trundle after him. How realistic and fun!

"We're in here," he says, stopping at a boardroom. A plaque says that on the door, anyway. Unlike the rest of the office, which is nothing but glass walls, this room has no windows looking in from the hallway.

He swings the door open and gestures for me to step inside. "Do you know how to take minutes, Ms. McLaughlin?"

"Yes, sir."

There's a pad of paper on the long, polished wood table, and he stops beside it for a moment, tapping his fingers on the surface. Then he nods. "Good."

He says it brusquely, and I like that.

Except I don't know how to take minutes, which isn't a big deal, except I realize there is a screen on the wall, and there is an actual person there. He's actually *holding a meeting.*

"Sam," I whisper, and he shoots me a look. It's hot and bossy and suggests I better not question him, so I grab the pad of paper and sit down.

As he starts talking to his client, I can't keep up with the back and forth, and it's all Sam's fault.

He's not paying me any attention at all, but somehow he's still riling me up. He's extra-big in his suit, his jaw is extra hard, and set at a *We'll-talk-about-this-later* angle that makes my thighs shake.

I find myself scribbling erotic story ideas instead of taking notes. The ideas are flying through my mind a mile a minute.

I try to focus. I try to be good.

I fail miserably.

Especially when he takes off his jacket and gets comfortable, rocking back in his chair. I can't see his legs under the table, but I imagine they're spread wide, his solid thighs flexing. His cock thick and heavy, right there. Out of reach, for now.

On one too-excited scribble, the pen rolls out of my fingers and lands on the floor. Sam shoots me that stern look and I mouth *sorry* at him. I'm a terrible secretary.

Maybe he'll spank me for this later.

I grin to myself as I push back and lean over to pick up the dropped pen. But my skirt is too tight, and it constricts my movement enough that I can't quite reach—I want to stretch my leg out to counterbalance my arm and upper body, but I can't. I roll back further and stand up carefully, trying to maintain the facade that I'm really Sam's assistant. I kneel carefully and reach for the pen—but stop, because underneath the table Sam is doing something incredibly filthy.

The jerk is rolling up his sleeves. The cuffs are undone already, and his fingers—those thick, strong digits that he likes to plunge into my body—are nimbly rolling the white cotton fabric up his forearm.

Slowly.

Carefully. With erotic precision.

As I take in deep, horny breaths, the ropes Sam bound me with an hour earlier press into my flesh.

How long is he going to torture me like this?

Seven more minutes, it turns out.

After I rescue my pen, he gets the client to agree to two key action items—which I actually do write down, go me— and then he ends the call.

My breath catches in my throat as he gets up and comes around the table. He looks at the notepad. I'm on the fourth page now, the others flipped up.

The page he's looking at has real work on it.

The others...not so much.

He grabs the pad and nods at what he sees. "Good."

That's not going to last long.

He flips to the previous page, then the one before that. "What is this?"

There's only one answer here. A lie. "The minutes of the meeting."

"His thighs brace against the luxurious leather seat, rock-hard

with tension as she uncrosses her legs. He wants to shove her skirt up and feast on her cun— Ms. McLaughlin, did you write this?"

"I—" I grab for the pad, and Sam catches my wrist in mid-air. He squeezes his fingers tight and slowly, threateningly pushes my hand back down to the table. I squeak and back up, my butt hitting the table, too. He leans in, forcing me to scoot back, hopping up onto the table to try to get away from his menacing approach.

And then he releases me and sits down in the leather chair I just vacated.

Now we're in exactly the position I just described. He's sitting down, his legs spread wide, framing his heavy erection. I'm perched on the boardroom table in front of him.

So I cross my legs.

Just so I can uncross them.

Sam's gaze narrows in on the shadow between my thighs.

My clit pulses, a desperate little slut. Ready to do anything, anywhere with this man. "What temp agency did you say you were from?"

His voice is full of gravel. Hot, intense.

"I don't remember."

"I think you came here to tempt me."

I did. I really did. "I tried my best, sir."

"You fantasized about me shoving your legs apart and burying my face in your hot, little cunt. Is that how you think of that sweet pussy between your legs? A needy, dripping cunt? Will you do anything for her?"

I can't breathe. "Yes."

"Show me."

My legs tremble. "Show you what?"

"Your cunt."

I try to ruck up my skirt, but it's too tight. Sam rears up, out of the chair, and shoves me onto my back. "I'll help."

He pushes the fabric up my thighs rough enough it hurts a little and turns me on a lot.

My thighs fall open, because I'm exactly as wanton as he accused me of being.

Sam leans in and tugs my panties to the side. He takes a long, slow sniff of my scent, which makes me shake in need, and then licks up one swollen pussy lip and down the other before slurping straight up the middle.

Slow, depraved, rabid licks.

Hungry, filthy.

Hot.

He wriggles his tongue against my clit at the end of each swipe, and when I buck my hips toward his face, he clamps a big hand on my thigh and presses me against the cool wood surface.

"Hold still," he barks.

Make me, I think.

And he does.

He pins me down, making it impossible for me to try to control the way his mouth works against my skin.

I want to scream and cry out, but I swallow that frustration and let go. Let go of my desire to rush to that orgasm, let go of the panicky edge, and sink into the feelings. Sam's ropes on my skin, his mouth between my legs.

I relinquish the last vestiges of any control I thought I had on this wild, erotic dream, and give in to what he is giving me.

Everything.

My orgasm grows like a bubble, glittering and wobbly. I feel it coming, getting bigger and bigger, and then, with a final hungry swipe of his tongue, Sam sends me flying, the bubble popping spectacularly.

"Good," Sam says, his face pressed against my inner thigh. He's breathing hard. "Very good." He stands up. "That will do for now. You should straighten up, our next meeting starts in fifteen minutes."

AFTER THE SECOND MEETING, I talk her into letting me unbutton her blouse, but I'm too rough and a few buttons go flying. I tug on the rope harness and pinch her breasts until she's squirming, and then I fuck her on my desk.

After the third meeting, I tell her I'm going to need her services all weekend, and she's going to have to stay with me in my apartment.

As she protests that she has other temp work to get to, I call us a cab.

It's started to rain buckets when we get outside.

"This is so much fun," she says as she waits under the overhang with me.

"The rain?"

"The role-play."

That pleases me more than I expected. "Is it as good as your fantasies?"

Her smile glitters in the waning light. "Better."

"How?"

"I don't know what you'll do next."

The surprise. I swallow around a very big feeling lodged in my throat. A regular occurrence with Hazel in my life. "We can do it again next month when we come back to the city. But different again, to keep you on your toes."

THREE WEEKS LATER, Hazel The Temp shows up at my office again. This time it's later in the day, because I want us to have dinner together. She's wearing a black suit, fitted pants and tailored blazer. She looks hot. The silky lingerie she's wearing under the jacket is even hotter.

"Ms. McLaughlin, we have a dress code. You've worked here before."

"This is all I have," she says softly. The demure act of a siren temptress.

"I remember a skirt last time. A blouse with buttons all the way to your neck."

"They're both ripped."

I don't think I tore the skirt, but the idea of it makes my cock hard. "Well, let's get started then. And if anyone comes in, you'll have to duck under the desk."

She beams at the idea.

Dirty little minx.

I pass her a pad of paper.

"Are you in meetings this evening again, sir?"

"Not today. Today we're going to—" I'm interrupted by my

phone vibrating on the desk. Right on schedule. I stand up and move closer to her, pressing my hands to her shoulders. "Let me help you get a bit more comfortable."

"You want me to take my jacket off?"

"I do," I whisper, grazing my fingers over the bare skin of her neck. "I like to look at you while we work."

"And what work are we doing today?"

"I want you to finish the story you started last time. What happens next after the cruel boss goes down on his secretary?"

"This isn't I was hired," she protests.

I tug her jacket off her shoulders and lean all the way over so I can lick her skin. "You were hired to keep me company on a late night. You were hired to be beautiful, and tempting, and when I need some relief, a tight little fuckhole."

She gasps.

And grins.

"Yes, sir."

"Now get writing."

Her pen flies across the page. I take her jacket and hang it up on the far side of the office, next to mine, then sit at my desk.

The elevator dings in the lobby, and Hazel jumps.

I gave her a bland look. *What are you going to do?*

Without missing a beat, she jumps up and scrambles under my desk. I protect her head with my hand as I roll my chair in closer. At the same time, I pull her face right against the erection tenting my pants. She wraps her hands around my legs as I pretend to do some work.

Alex strolls in. "It's a good thing I was already coming downtown for the show," he says. "Asking me to play delivery boy is a bit rich."

"Sorry, man." I give him a grateful smile. "You know how it is. I need to get this done before tonight. But I'll see you there, because you brought me sustenance. And now I can power through this."

He gives me a suspicious look, but waves and takes his leave.

Hazel presses her face against my thigh and quietly laughs as I listen for the elevator to depart again. Then I get up and close my office door.

I lock it, too, for good measure.

She's curled up in my chair when I turn around. "That was definitely unexpected. I'm surprised you didn't have me blow you while I was down there."

"I have to feed you, first," I growl, hauling her out of my chair. Then I pull her back into my lap once I'm seated again.

"Does Alex know I'm here?"

"Nope. I knew he was coming in this direction for a show tonight, and I asked him if he could pick me up some food from a place I like near his house which famously does not deliver."

"Sneaky." She squares her shoulders. "What would you like me to do next, Mr. Preston?"

"Eat. And then we're going out."

Hazel's eyes go wide. "Sam…"

"Yes?"

"I'm not dressed for going out."

I pull a present from my bottom desk drawer. A slim box. Inside it is a long, silk scarf. Red. "You can wear this. It can be tied as a halter top under your jacket."

She bites her lip. "So the night is not over when we leave here?"

I draw her in close, enveloping her in my arms. Holding her tight. "The night is just beginning."

"How exciting." Her eyes sparkle.

"I'm glad you think so. Now, bend over the desk."

She stands, and I unbutton her pants. As she folds in half, I tug them down her hips, revealing the pale swell of her ass divided by the thong of her sexy lingerie body suit. I trace the fabric down her crack, rubbing against her slit before I raise my hand again.

"This is reward," I tell her before I bring my palm down with a light slap.

"For what, sir?"

"For being adventurous."

"Oh…" She exhales. "Thank you."

Two words that go straight to my soul. I warm her bottom up, left and right, back and forth, and then tell her she's earned six very good, very stingy taps.

She wriggles in anticipation.

I deliver them quickly, my heart pounding. One, two, three. Fuck she likes this so much. Four, five, six. My cock aches, but I don't want to fuck her here. Not tonight.

I want to save that for the end of the night—after all of my surprises.

25

HAZEL

It's a lovely night, unseasonably warm, so we walk from Sam's office. I'm tightly wrapped in the red silk scarf he got me, and if I don't take off my blazer, it functions perfectly as an acceptable outfit for being in public.

Also hidden from public view is my tender bum. Sam makes sure to brush up against where he paddled me, though. He's thoughtful like that.

We head west, my boyfriend completely mum about where we are going. Instead, Sam's talking about home renovations, and I'm only listening with half an ear. "What do you think about that?"

"About what?"

"Going back to the lodge next Christmas."

It's March. I don't plan my life out that far, but I like the idea of it. "Sure."

"I know you don't like to plan that far in advance."

I laugh. "You read my mind."

"But I thought we should maybe lock in those dates. Just to be on the safe side."

"Does it matter when we go?"

"Well…" Sam stops in the shadow of a theatre, the marquee lights dazzling behind him. "I had an idea."

"Are we going to a show?"

He glances behind him. "Yes, but not that one."

"Oh, a clue."

"Hazel."

"Sam."

"Can I have your full and undivided attention for a minute?" He grins at me, and tugs me along, past the theatre.

"Where are we going?"

"It's a surprise. But I want to ask you something first. It's about houses. Yours, and mine, and if we should keep both, and how much time we should spend in them. How we spend time in them."

He stops again at the next street, dodges around a group of pedestrians, and pulls me onto a quieter side street.

"Hazel, I'm trying to say, I want to be with you. All the time, and for always. From the moment we re-connected, I haven't wanted to leave your side. And this is coming out all wrong, but I love working on your house with you. I love having you in my house. And I want to have a conversation about what *you* want, what you love, so we can be on the same page."

"I…" He wants my full and undivided attention for this conversation, so I'm taking it seriously. I'm thinking about it. "I love both homes, too. If you don't mind going back and forth, I don't, either. And there are some real advantages to living in the city. The naughty office role-play, for example. And that theatre. We could go see a live show. That would be great. Are you worried that I'm going to want you to move to Stratford?"

"I—I was hoping you might. Want something like that, I mean."

"Oh." I let that sink in. "Sam, I love you so much. I really do. I don't care where we live. If you want to keep a place in the city, because it's easier for work…"

He had talked about leaving the investment firm behind, but something is stopping him. And that's his choice to make, when it's right for him.

"Well, the question is a little more personal than that. Because I want to buy you something. A promise ring, of sorts. But it's a bit bigger than a ring. Too big, in fact, for your house. And if you like it, we might need to keep my apartment in order to keep the gift. I thought about surprising you with it, but I didn't want you to think I was trapping you in the city." He tugs me against him. "As much as I do like trapping you, I like it even more when we've discussed it in advance, in at least the broadest of strokes."

I'm speechless. Not just because of the mystery gift, but all the rest of it. *A promise ring, of sorts.* It's so innocently sweet, it takes my breath away.

"Is it—"

Sam touches his finger to my lips. "Don't try to guess. We'll be there soon. A few more blocks."

I lace my fingers through his. "Then lead on."

❋

IT'S AN ART GALLERY. And I recognize one of the names on the poster in the window.

"Grace is having a show?"

Sam opens the door for me, and a hum of noise floods out. "It's a VIP preview. The show opens next week."

"This is where Alex was going!" I wave at Sam's friend, and then with both hands at Grace, who I spot just past him. "Why didn't you tell…"

That's when I see it.

I know before he says anything that the twelve-foot-tall birdcage is mine, if I want it. If I will accept it from Sam. "That's why," I whisper.

He rubs his hand in the small of my back. "Do you want to go and see it up close? It creaks delightfully."

I'm going to cry.

I don't know why, but I'm going to make an embarrassing mess of myself in a moment. I turn into his chest and press my forehead against his body.

"Do you like it?"

"I love it." I drag in a deep breath and compose myself. When I look back, the crowd has parted, and we head in that direction. I stop halfway to congratulate Grace, but someone else grabs her, and then I'm free to move all the way to the back of the gallery.

"This isn't Grace's work, is it?"

Sam stops right behind me, his arm tight around my waist.

"No. One of the other artists. A metal worker named Damien Noble."

"Even if I hadn't already agreed to go back and forth, I would move to the city to live with this."

Sam laughs. "And me."

"And you. Of course, and you." I look up at him. "Who else would put me in this cage and let me write?"

His eyes flare, and his mouth tightens.

I school my features into delightful innocence. "How soon can we get it home?"

"They'll deliver it after the exhibit."

"Which ends…"

"In three weeks." He drops a slow, promising kiss on my mouth. "But I have another surprise waiting for you at home."

Home.

I can picture it. Making his loft a little more me, a little more us. This birdcage in the corner. I'm not kidding about wanting to write in it, maybe curled up on a velvet cushion.

Tearing myself away from the cage, I turn my attention to the other pieces by the metal worker. "This is all so very, very…kinky," I whisper to Sam.

"There's a reason for that," he murmurs back. "The show was put together by the club owner you saw at Alex's on New Year's Eve. He was there to meet Grace."

"What?"

Sam shifts my body until Zeke Devereaux is in my line of sight.

This night just gets better and better.

"Do you know him?"

"Never met the man. But we have a card for his club, surely that's as good an ice breaker as any?"

I'm blushing. I know I am. We'd decided not to go the club, not yet. We are having fun figuring out our own kinky play. But now I'm surrounded by it all, and someone I've followed online—a genuine star in this world—is right there.

And I no longer need to pretend I don't know who he is.

"I might embarrass myself," I mutter.

Sam squeezes my still-tender bottom. "Maybe he likes that sort of thing."

But I don't embarrass myself, and Zeke is a completely cool, non-creepy professional the whole conversation.

I'm buzzing hard as we find Grace and make our good-byes, when I see Sam's brother step through the front door.

He looks awkward and out of place, but more than anything, he looks tired. He joins us, or at least joins Grace, giving her a quick kiss in greeting.

The way she looks at him slays me, like she wants so much more than that, and would give him anything if he'd see it. They have so many troubles and I barely know any of it.

Sam has tensed way up, too. New goal: get him out of here without him and Luke exchanging words.

But I'm not that smooth about it, because as soon as we're outside, Sam calls me on it. "You don't need to run interference with him."

"Maybe I was hustling you out of there for my own reasons?" I wrinkle my nose. "But I wasn't. I just didn't like how you tensed up. That's all."

"He loves Grace," Sam says. "In his own way. Just when I

think he doesn't, he shows up like this and I think, maybe this time it'll be different."

I hold out my hand.

I don't have anything smart to say there. But I can hold Sam's hand as he hails a cab so we can go home.

Together.

26

SAM

WHEN WE GET HOME, I unwind the silk scarf from Hazel, then help her get undressed. But instead of leading her into the shower, or to the bed—our bed, now—I take her back to the living room.

All the lights are out in the apartment. We move through the dark space, lit only by the glow of the city outside, to where I think we'll put the birdcage.

"Right here," I whisper to her. "This is where I'll decorate your birdcage in tapestries and ropes."

"I want a velvet cushion." She sways against me.

"We'll get you a pile of them." I press her against the brick wall. Gently. Roughly. Both at the same time, exactly as she likes it. "Imagine yourself tied open for my leisure exploration."

"Oh, I'm picturing it."

I nuzzle my face into her neck. "Would you write about it?"

"Absolutely."

"Ice giant?"

"Dragon," she says immediately. "With big, rough fingers."

I tighten my grip on her side. "And who is his love?"

"Someone who feels safer when she's bound."

"His wife, maybe?"

She makes a thinking sound. "I probably wouldn't write it like that."

"This isn't your story anymore. It's ours." I inhale the sweet scent of her, then slide down to one knee. "What about you, Hazel? Would you be my wife? Let me keep you safe forever?"

She inhales sharply, and it's foolish to do this in the dark, when I can't see her face properly, but then I lift the ring into the faint light, and the gold rope strands and the brilliant diamond glitter.

"You make me feel whole," I tell her. "And nothing brings me more joy than being an earnest partner for you. To explore life and love with you would be the greatest gift."

"Oh, Sam." She reaches her fingers out, pale and delicate, and gasps again as she touches the ring. "Yes. I want that, too."

"Will you marry me, then?"

"Yes." She nods and falls into my arms. "Yes."

I cradle her against my body and sink to the floor. *Yes.*

THE BIRDCAGE IS DELIVERED three weeks later, while we're in Stratford. I don't tell Hazel, and the thrill of that surprise, the deep, intoxicating secret, makes me realize that I am not merely following her happily through this kink exploration we are on.

I am all in. I am a dirty fucking bastard.

She has no idea how deeply it pleases me to hold her captive. To know it is my choice if she is ever allowed to leave.

At least on some level—until she safe words out, which we've started to talk about, too.

I am jacked up with excitement when we head back that night. It has to show in how handsy I am, how fucking horny I am for Hazel, but she doesn't let on if she has realized something is up.

She's talking about some piece she read on the news when we walk into the loft.

She stops talking immediately when she sees it.

It's dark outside, the loft full of shadows, but the shape of it is clear. I swear we can smell it, too. Bare metal. Greased up hinges on that door.

But I got her the velvet cushions she wanted, too.

She breathes my name as she twists into my arms. I lift her up, holding her tight, and carry her across the room. Our bags are forgotten at the door.

All that matters is this. My fiancée in my arms, the way she shivers when I open the birdcage door. The way she hesitates when I set her down and order her to undress.

Her hesitation thrills me, too.

I grip my hand around a bar, blocking the doorway. "Hazel."

She twirls away. "I love it," she says dreamily. "It's just so much."

"I want to take you here. Now." I follow her in, the door clanging shut behind me.

Hazel slides off her shirt.

I watch, gaze hooded, as she peels off her clothes. When she's naked, I put my hand on her shoulder. Heavy. Commanding. I push her to her knees, remembering what she said to me our first night together. I should have known then, and maybe I did on some level, but nothing like this.

I didn't understand how powerful this could be. For her to ask me to force her, to share this fantasy.

To make this fantasy a reality for the woman I love.

"Do you like your cushions?"

She wriggles on them. "Yes. They're beautiful."

"Good. Make sure you stay on them. If any part of you gets bruised tonight, I want it to be from my hand, not the floor."

She swallows hard. "Understood."

I unzip, then grab her hair. She opens for me, her mouth eager and wet, and I thrust in deep. This is just the start. I'm going to fuck her next. There's an A to Z encyclopedia of ways to love her in this cage, against this cage. We're going to explore all of them in time.

But right now, I want to claim her. Fast, hard, rough.

When my cock is as hard as it's going to get—fucking throbbing—I pull out and kneel in front of her. I kiss her so hard it might feel punishing, but she makes the sweetest sound against my tongue, my lips. So God damned happy to take everything I give her.

"Hold on to the cage," I growl at her, and lift her by her hips.

She gasps and clutches the bars behind her as I plunge into her tender pussy. We fucked earlier, and she's still swollen from that. I knew this was coming, too, but I was too excited to wait.

Fuck.

Her pussy clenches around me as I bottom out, threatening to milk me before we even begin.

"This is going to be fast," I warn her. "I need you to come for me."

She whines.

"That noise isn't going to keep me from spilling myself inside you before you get there. That noise just makes me want to use you."

"Please please yes. Use me," she whispers.

I won't. Not ever. I'll make it perfect for her every time, but that's not the fantasy. I tighten my grip on one hip, and slide the other hand across her belly, over her mound. I love the plump top of her slit, where her clit nestles and gets hard when she's turned on.

It's a throbbing bump right now, tall and proud, and slicked up already with her pussy juice. So fucking hot. I rock my thumb left to right, a slow roll that always gives her the pressure she likes. She grinds against the touch and whimpers again.

"Needy girl. Get yourself off, because I'm almost there. My little captive slut. Next time I'll tie you up so you can't squirm so much."

She cries out at that, her whole body clenching up, and I thunder my hips home, fucking into her in three more jerky thrusts before I follow her into an orgasm that makes spots appear in my vision.

"Oh. Sam..." Hazel breathes.

Fuck, yeah. "That's it." I'm breathing so hard. "Say my name."

She laughs. "My cocky beloved. I'll say your name forever."

THE NEXT MORNING, I wake up alone. I can smell coffee, but Hazel never gets up before me. Stretching, I go in search of her.

She's in her cage. She has a big cup of coffee on a little table she's pulled in there, and she's writing on her computer. I leave her to it, and go in search of the coffee she's made.

Maybe I'll sit on the couch for a while and just watch her being wonderful.

EPILOGUE
SAM

Christmas, again

THE WOMAN across from me on the train is lost in concentration, hard at work.

It would be rude of me to interrupt her and tell her how beautiful she is. How much she reminds me of my university crush, the secret fantasy that got me through the last term of school when my life was falling apart—the second time, and not the last time.

I really should let my wife get her work done. We have a week of honeymoon ahead of us, after all.

"I can hear your thoughts from here," she mutters. "I'm almost done."

"I didn't say anything." I grin.

"You didn't need to. I know I promised no work on this trip, but…"

I know. But Grace asked for Hazel's help. "It's fine. I like watching you do your thing. Concentration is very sexy."

Her lips twitch, and she finally looks up. "Can I give you one of your gifts early? It's something to read."

I sit up straighter. I have a bracelet for her in my pocket. "Great idea."

She leans over and pulls a thin rectangle from her backpack. It's light and feels like paper when she hands it over.

I dig out the jewellery box and pass it across to her. "And for you, my beloved."

A soft, glorious smile crosses her face. "Merry Christmas."

I wait for her to go first, and she makes a lovely sound when she opens the box. It's a gold rope bracelet that matches her ring—a reminder, and a promise.

"It's stunning." She holds out her wrist so I can put it on her, then she gestures at my gift. "Now your turn."

I carefully peel the paper away.

It's a book. A slim volume, and my guess is that it may be the only copy in existence.

A collection of poems inspired by Sam Preston

"A limited edition binding?" I read the subtitle out loud.

"Very limited," she says softly. "For your eyes only."

My suspicion was correct.

"An excellent gift," I say around the thick knot in my throat, tighter than any I've used on her. "And a perfect distraction."

She climbs out of her seat and leans over to kiss me. "I'll be quick," she promises. "And then we can play a game for the last leg of the trip."

"When will I find out what this secret is that you and Grace are working on together?"

She shrugs. "I don't know. When she's ready to share it with the world. Which might be next week, or it might not be for months."

I let it go and lean back in my seat. I have a precious book to read, a glass of whiskey to sip, and a half-empty train car with nobody around.

HAZEL

When Sam goes back to his drink, and the chapbook I had printed just for him, I look at the most recent email Grace sent me.

I'm okay. Or I will be. Please don't tell Sam. I don't want to ruin your time away. I'm sorry you found out like that.

She has nothing to be sorry for. That's all on her husband.

I glance across the table at my own husband. Half-brother to the man Grace loves, for reasons I cannot wrap my head around.

Sam will kill Luke when he finds out, so it's my job to make sure he never does.

Thank you so much for reading *Tempt*! Turn the page to read some of Hazel's poems about Sam, and details about the next book in this duet, *Shame*, which will conclude the story of the Preston family!

A COLLECTION OF POEMS INSPIRED BY SAM PRESTON

LIMITED EDITION BINDING

The sounds I imagine you make
by Aibhlin Moon

A growly burr
A slow fade into exhalation
A groan
A gasp

When I'm on my knees
Or above you, head curved low

Beneath you, shifting
As you pin my arms against the bed

I would love to wring your pleasure
In a thousand ways

As the sounds I imagine you make
Get me every time

The sounds you make, my beloved
by Aibhlin Moon

Before I knew the sounds you made
I wondered, dreamed

I fantasized of grunts and growls
Illicit acts rendered in song

But the sounds you make, my beloved
Are better than that

A soft exhale
A warm groan in sleep

When you're holding me close
A heavy arm against my side

A heady hiss
A teasing whisper

When you press me open
And kiss me deep

The sounds you make, my beloved
Are glorious and giving

The sounds I make
by Aibhlin Moon

You heard my dreams before I spoke
My secret wants

And in my pause, in that brief space
You saw a thing, a spark, a crave

Please bind my heart, so I can cry
Please press me down, so I can fly

Please
Ouch
Ah

Sounds I make, because you love me
Secrets kept, because you love me

Pleasure unbound by common rules
Serves uncommon love

Love
The sound I make for my husband

GRACE'S BOOK IS NEXT
PRE-ORDER SHAME TODAY

Shame is a novel three years in the making. Many will think it's not a romance, and maybe it's not. But it is a story carefully told to ensure that one character—Grace—gets everything she wants and more.

Shame will release in March 2021.

Content warnings and pre-order links on my website:
ainsleybooth.com/secrets-and-lies-duet/

Turn the page to get inside Grace and Luke's heads for the first time.

GRACE:

I never thought my husband would cheat on me. I was wrong.
Now I need to pick up the tattered remnants of my life and
figure out how to put one foot in front of the other. How to
look at myself in the mirror without seeing my own secrets
scrawled there in shameful scarlet.

LUKE:

I am exactly the asshole you think I am.

I don't deserve her. I should walk away. But I can't let her go
without a fight. Too late—too damn late—I'm realizing what
I've done and everything that I've lost. Everything I want back
again, or maybe really to have and to hold properly for the
first time. In order to stay with Grace and win her back, I'm
going to need to storm through fire, over and over again.

If you like silly, sexy, over the top fairy tale romances…
Billionaire Secrets

Undercover Billionaire
Her Billionaire Best Friend
A Billionaire for Christmas

Coming soon in this series…
Shame

And in the same world…
Crave

Want to know more?
www.ainsleybooth.com

ABOUT THE AUTHOR

Ainsley Booth a three-time USA Today bestselling author of erotic romance. Between her two pen names (she also writes contemporary romance as two-time New York Times bestseller Zoe York), she has published more than fifty books since 2013. Notable hits include *Prime Minister* and *Hate F*@k*.

9 781989 703809